Dead End
Ride

A Lieutenant Beaudry novel

MEZZO PUBLICATIONS Inc.

Montreal, Canada

Copyright © 2022 All rights reserved.

BOOK ISBN-13: 978-1-7771314-3-2

ELECTRONIC BOOK ISBN-13: 978-1-7771314-4-9

Cover art Mary60-Design

DEDICATED TO

The fans of Lieutenant Beaudry, and to all mystery and thriller novel readers.

ACKNOWLEDGMENTS

My thanks to my Beta readers and supporters, Patricia Bernier, Judith Leaper, Hank Sherrard, Charles Robitaille, and Sin De Barnwell for their continued support. And to fellow authors, Jim Napier, Randall Krzak, and Del Chatterson for their insights, suggestions, and reviews.

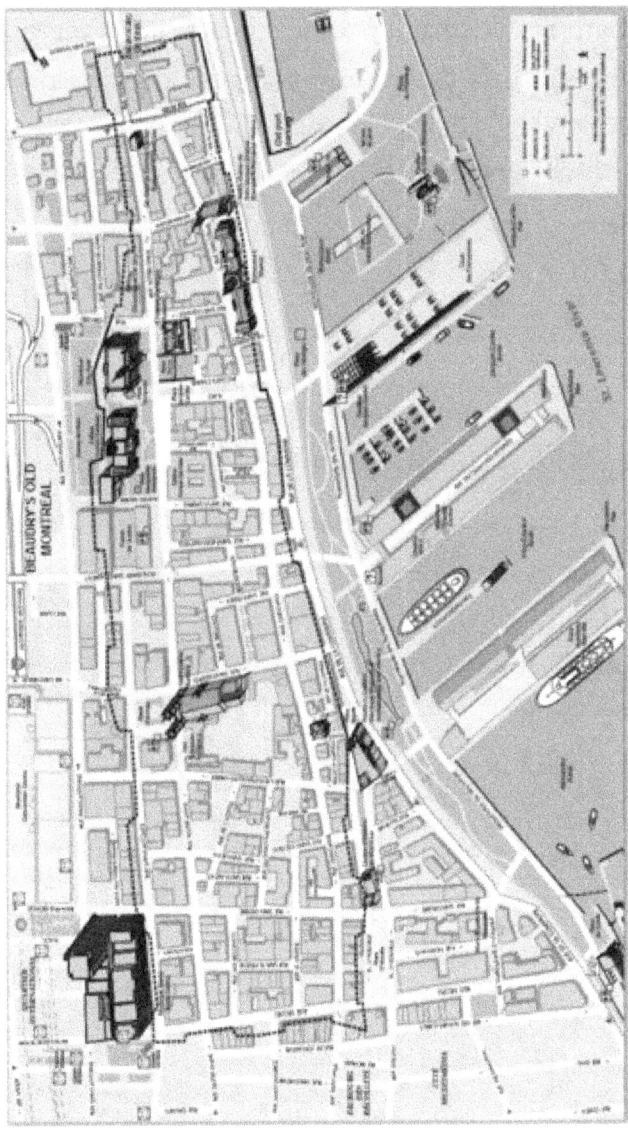

A path that turns out to be a dead end is very useful because you don't devote resources to focusing on that; you go elsewhere

~ Michael Bloomberg[1]

---

1.   https://www.inspiringquotes.us/author/7078-michael-bloomberg

ONE

I'm a homicide detective. To investigate a murder, there must be a corpse, preferably, with some evidence of foul play. At seven twelve a.m. I was with a forensic investigator in a patch of marshland at the limit of a dead-end road. I stood uncomfortably among waist-high grass and cattails; smelly water slowly seeped into my old Wellington boots.

It was an early spring morning, that time of year when the sun starts off lazy. The sunrise showed a radiant blue sky, but a deceitful breeze brought an uncomfortable chill and a musty smell to our surroundings. I should have worn a sweater under my light jacket this morning, but I knew by lunchtime I'd be peeling it off.

Sargent Tristan Dobson led me to a badly charred motorcycle. I've worked with him for the last six years. He's our top lab technician in the Forensic Identification Service, Montreal's equivalent of CSI.

With his large tortoiseshell eyeglasses, spiky hair, mild stutter, and hesitant speech, he resembles the typical lab nerd from a Hollywood comedy movie.

His non-standard attire for today didn't help his image. He wore an old ragged green and beige striped sweater over his white crime scene coveralls. The only people who know he's not a nerd—and fear him, are defense attorneys. He's a perfectionist who regularly finds a telling clue that most other techs miss, and that often incriminates the suspect. Until this morning, he was my favorite go-to person for help with my cases.

"Why am I wasting a bright sunny Wednesday morning in a swamp looking at a burned-out motorcycle?"

"Be-because it's a murder scene," Dobson said.

"There's no body. No body, no murder."

"Three feet to the right of the handlebars, there's a large patch of brown moss. Everywhere else the moss is a light springtime pale green. Green and red make yellow, or b-brown if the mix is high on the red side. I'd guess it took at least eight pints of blood to stain that spot," Dobson said.

"Doesn't mean we have a dead body. I still don't have a job to do, Tristan."

"The average male body contains ten to twelve pints of blood. If you lose forty percent of your blood, you die. He w-was gutted here. I wanted you to see the kill scene."

"He? A male body?"

Dobson reached into his backpack and pulled out a transparent evidence bag with a single lightly singed man-sized leather glove.

"Okay, you got me interested. Who called this in?"

"A local ornithologist. This area is, t-the best birdwatching site on the island with more than a hundred and ninety different species of birds spotted last season."

"Not into birds. I'm into evidence. Who was the caller?" I said.

"Left the location data and hung up. A cell phone on the Rogers network, no other info."

My right foot was now enveloped in a wet squishy sock. I moved out of the damp mossy area onto a rocky patch.

I said, "Can you give me a thread of actual evidence to hang on to?"

"As soon as the photographer finishes, we'll bring the bike to the lab. Everything is charred, b-but I'll give you the registered owner from the plate and VIN."

From the other side of the bike, the young photographer skirted around the dark patch of earth and sidled up to me. The breeze had cranked up another notch teasing her shoulder-length, near-white, blonde hair across her freckled face. She looked up at me with wide blue eyes as she swept errant strands from her mouth.

I gave her my best little boy smile.

"You're Lieutenant Beaudry, aren't you?"

"Last time I looked at my ID card, that's what I read."

"Now, I know why they call you 'Fridge'. You're very square and muscly."

"I try to keep in shape. I was on my way to the gym when Dobson called me."

She smiled demurely, while giving me a sly once-over glance.

To hide my shoulder rig, I had dressed in a summer-weight light gray linen sports jacket over a tight pale-blue T-shirt and black jeans.

I earned my "fridge" nickname from years of weight training and boxing. I recently added Tai Chi to give me more flexibility.

"You nearly finished here?" I said.

"Just getting started. I must take a few hundred pictures at a crime scene. We have only one chance to document everything and get all the details on file before they move the physical evidence."

Even though her face claimed eighteen, I guessed her age at around twenty-four. I deduced from her rote comment that she must have just finished the police academy and was now under the tutelage of Tristan.

"I've captured everything I need in my head," I said. "If I missed anything, I'm sure I'll find it in the file. I'm headed back on the road now. Dobson is the best coach you can get. Good luck with the new job."

Her blue eyes went wider.

"I'm sure we'll find the body," she said. "This was a dead-end ride for somebody."

I smiled at her and walked toward Dobson.

He was on his knees, examining a slender cattail leaf. His white coveralls were now camouflaged with mud spots and brambles. He plucked something from it with a pair of surgical tweezers. He stood up and showed me a long hair dangling from his shiny tool. He said, "The devil is in the details."

"Call me when you're finished with your inventory," I said. "I can't open a murder book until you find a body, but I'll make some calls and poke around unofficially once you give me a name to go with the bike."

He gave me a thumbs-up sign. I sloshed my way back to my Jeep. I changed my shoes and headed to the gym.

TWO

I had finished my routine and was wiping down the bench when my friend from the other side of the badge walked up. The gym owner Antonio was an ex-enforcer for a New York mob. After federal agents rounded his bosses up and sent them on a long vacation behind bars, he promptly, and wisely, retired. He moved to Montreal and used his ill-gotten funds to buy a French bistro and this gym.

"You're late this morning. Is this a day off?"

"Nope, still going nowhere on an old case, and I spent a few early hours in a swamp looking at the remnants of a Harley chopper."

"A new murder?"

"The tech guy thinks so. Lots of blood on the scene."

"No body?"

"Nope."

"Speaking of motorcycles, I had a drink with the leader of a bike club on Monday. He told me that one of his clan was missing as of last Saturday," Antonio said.

"This doesn't sound like a coincidence. Tell me more."

"I'm retired, but I like to keep in the know of what's happening in my ex-world. The biker gang has criminal connections."

My raised eyebrows and turned down mouth must have given him a hint of my discomfort. He didn't need to give me an explanation, but he did.

"A total awareness of my environment has kept me alive until now," he said. "I'd like to keep it that way. I have to know if anything of potential danger or of criminal intrigue is happening in town."

"What's the missing guy's name?" I said.

"I only got 'Flash' as his nickname. Do you want me to inquire?"

"Best not to at this point. I should get an I.D. on the bike's owner from the lab soon."

As I headed to the showers. Antonio said, "Keep me in the loop, Robert."

* * *

I had made a small dent in the pile of late reports moldering on my desk. It wouldn't tip the scales of justice in favor of the good guys, but it would keep the paper-pushing brass happy.

My boss of Irish descent must have tagged a leprechaun in his youth and somehow gained psychic abilities. I can sneak in to headquarters making less noise than a spider, but never without him knowing. About to head for lunch, I had just left my seat when my phone rang. The little screen announced his extension number. I answered my usual, "Beaudry, talk to me."

"My office." Was the instruction before the dial tone clicked in.

Chief inspector O'Neil's door was always open. I turned into his office and remained standing, hoping for a fast escape.

It was fast, but not an escape.

"What's up?" I said. "I was just going to lunch. Do you want me to bring you back a fresh coffee?"

The little gray fuzzy mustache that resided under his pug nose was straight. For him, it was the equivalent of a smile.

"That would be nice, but you won't have time. One of the short-term parking attendants at the airport found a smelly body in the trunk of a car. Today's detectives are out, or at lunch. It's yours. Get to it."

"Okay. I'll eat at the airport."

* * *

By the time I got to Trudeau airport, I was starving. I figured to take a fast peek at the victim, then find a restaurant with a decent menu before the FIS tech team got involved. The best laid plans of mice and men, yadda, yadda, yadda. It preempted my lunch. The crime scene analysts were on the spot when I arrived. The lead technician was someone new to me. A tall prim lady with gray streaks in her chestnut hair. Her ribboned bun and lanky stance reminded me of my fourth grade and favorite teacher, Madame Helene. I clipped my badge to my neck lanyard as I approached. It broke my memories of the old schoolhouse when I saw her stern and unhappy face. I read Anna Lakatos on her name tag. Her four-person team was in disposable white, polypropylene hooded coveralls. She pointed me to the tech van.

"Suit up."

"I'm not getting close to the body. I just need a fast peek."

"No contamination near my site. Suit up."

"Yes, ma'am."

* * *

She gave me a disapproving look when I glanced into the car trunk,

"The overalls are too tight around my shoulders. I can't zip up more than halfway," I said.

She shook her head and sighed loudly.

"Get on with it. Make it fast. Touch nothing."

"Yes, ma'am."

The man was on his back, hands tucked behind him and his knees pushed up against his torso. His face and lips were Oxiclean white with a light blue tinge.

His throat was slit, the left carotid severed. He was in what looked like new jeans cinched with a black leather belt closed with a Harley logo buckle. He wore a scarred black leather jacket over what had been a bright yellow T-shirt. The left side of the jacket, T-shirt and the same side leg of the jeans were stained dark brown. The color of dried blood.

As I backed away from the Camry, I pulled out my notebook and pen.

"Any identification from the car or the body?"

She flipped a few pages back on her clipboard.

"Wallet was in his jacket. The picture on the driver's permit card matches the victim."

I nodded toward the Camry.

"I hope his photo looks better than this."

She ignored my inane remark and continued her inventory list.

"Notation for Class 5 vehicles and 6A for big engine motorcycles for a Mr. Frank Diorio. Three hundred and eighty-five dollars in bills. Six fifty-five in change. A Mastercard issued to the same name. The car was a weekend rental from Enterprise here at the airport to a Miss Monica Tubbs, a New York-driving permit."

The efficient but unsmiling Anna gave me an address on Felix Leclerc in the borough of Saint Laurent for Mr. Diorio. It was just north of the airport, close to the wooded area where we found the bike. Another coincidence, I didn't think so. I gave her my card, and she texted me a copy of the rental contract for the Camry, as well as Diorio's driving permit.

I thanked her and headed for lunch. The next steps in the investigation were up to me.

THREE

There are only a few restaurants in the airport prior to the secure boarding zone. I suffered a mediocre meal at a hamburger stand. I added a side salad and fried onions to the soft drink and French fries trio. I'd have to find time to do a longer gym session tomorrow.

When my phone played its jazz tune, I took my last bite of the overcooked double beef burger. As I fished it out of my jacket, Tristan Dobson's funny semi-inebriated grin was on the screen. When Pat and I moved in together, I had taken this picture at the housewarming party. I met Pat on a murder case nearly three years ago. I had been smitten by her redhead Irish good looks, her quick repartee, and her police skills.

Her uncle, my boss, Chief inspector Jean O'Neil, had gone to Dublin for his brother's funeral and come back with niece Patricia in tow. She had been an officer in the Garda, Ireland's police service. She did her police work shifts and cared for her stubborn, "I want to die in-my-home" dad during what they diagnosed as a stage-IV pancreatic cancer. The work, care and worry had emptied her. Both of her brothers had left Dublin years before, her mother, passed many years ago in childbirth, Pat, would have been living alone in the old family home with the ghosts of her parents. Jean convinced her to take a couple of months off and vacation in Canada.

Of course, Pat being Pat, the vacation turned into going to the police academy in Nicolet. She graduated with flying colors and joined our fraud squad five years ago. After a divorce from a sweet-talking but unscrupulous lawyer, she did a stint in homicide that led to our meeting. Our case had been a violent one with a lot of gun play. A bullet wound to her leg prompted her to go back to her original Fraud Squad job.

I was still in awe that such a smart and beautiful woman would fall for a big, over-muscled lug like me.

I answered the call. "Talk to me."

"I have the info from the bike's registration," Dobson said.

"I'll bet you a bottle of good Spanish Rioja Reserva, that his name is Frank Diorio," I said.

"Un, unbelievable. No wonder you've got the best case solved record ever."

"Just luck on this one, my friend. I caught a dead body in the trunk of a car at Trudeau airport. I met Anna Lakatos, a tech I didn't know. She found his wallet."

"Too m-many vacations on our staff. She's on loan from the SQ. Was the body gutted?"

"I'm surprised that our Provincial Police are that generous. Yes, he had bled out. He was as pale as Casper, the Ghost. His throat was slit from just below his right ear to the left severed carotid, a clean cut. His hands were tied behind his back. When I got there, she hadn't moved the victim yet."

"What was the wine bet?"

"Never mind Tristan, I was just joking with you. I'll be on the road. Call me if there's anything new."

Since I had my phone in hand, I called Antonio. As usual, it went to his answering service. He'd take my message and reply in the next hour. He survived in a business where you normally get retired without a gold watch. Usually it was a bullet or a garotte. He was overly cautious, to the point of near invisibility.

I decided to check out victim Diorio's digs. I headed northeast to his address. I didn't have a search warrant yet, nor would I bother getting one. On the street, I've often found that building supervisors and landlords are very helpful. They much prefer a discreet inquiry by one big cop than a dozen uniforms clomping around in the building. Apparently, it worries the tenants. These days, people just don't want any branch of government peeking around their homes or their lives. As if the software on their computer and phone isn't recording their every message and move. It's the invasion of the invisible nongovernment that should worry them, not our blue uniforms.

As I turned onto Diorio's street, my radio muted, killing "Lovers in Paris" from Jacob Gurevitsch. Antonio's gravelly voice replaced my favorite melody.

"You called me. I'm listening." Was his usual brusque response to a phone message.

"You asked me to keep you in the loop," I said.

"So."

"The motorcycle's owner is Frank Diorio. They found his body in the trunk of a rental car at the airport this morning. Throat sliced cleanly."

"Looks like a message from a professional," Antonio said.

"We agree. If the 'Flash' nickname ties in with Diorio, can you get me a meeting with the gang leader?" I said. "Everything will be off the record."

He hung up after saying, "Call you back."

FOUR

It was a short safari to hunt down the building supervisor. I found him in the lobby entrance, helping a locksmith repair the glass door's electric lock.

He was a skinny Asian of indeterminate age. Pure white short-hair, and a pink scar starting from the bottom of his left ear up to his cheek bone.

I did my signature left-handed open the leather badge holder flip. His face soured when he saw the gold shield.

"I just need a word with you. Off the record."

A hesitant smile softened his pissed off look. He slid through the half-opened door and motioned me into the hallway. The locksmith had to get off his knees and open it wider to let me enter. I wasn't making many friends this morning. It would probably get worse when I'd tell him the reason for my visit.

It didn't.

"Your tenant in two-o-six will not be paying his rent this month. He's been murdered. I'd need a fast look in his apartment. I don't have a search warrant. Didn't think I'd need one. But it's easily done in a homicide case. This is just between you and me. If you don't want twenty policemen clopping around in your building, we may avoid it—if you and I visit together, now."

Shaking his head slowly. He studied the floor for a few seconds, a sad look on his kisser.

"Murdered, not good. A hungry ghost," he said softly.

"Murder is not good in any tradition," I said. "I will give him peace by finding his killer. He'd thank you for helping me."

He looked up with the hint of a smile on his lips.

"My name is Huizhong," he said.

17

I saluted him army style. "Robert."

It got me a wider smile and a fast entry into the apartment.

* * *

He stood a respectful five or six feet behind me as I walked through Diorio's place. It wasn't immaculate, but it was clean. I took visual notes, touching nothing in the apartment. I doubted that I'd find any clues to the killer's identity here.

The only unmanly items in the apartment were several lipstick and mascara tainted tissues in the washroom wastebasket.

I turned to Huizhong.

"He has a lady friend?"

"Too many. Other tenants complain. Nights, many laughs, many yells."

I thanked my shadow partner and left the building not much wiser than when I had entered. Before my departure, I had mentioned that some lab people may also want to inspect the apartment. I told him I didn't need more than our brief visit.

* * *

When Antonio called back, I was headed to my favorite food emporium.

"Yup, Frank is the missing biker. My guy will meet you late tonight at my bistro."

"Pat is at home cramming for an exam. I'm cooking supper tonight," I said. "Tomorrow, preferably not in a public place. A cop and a criminal together, not good for my, or his reputation."

"Tomorrow, the gym, an hour before official opening."

"I'm good with that. Was Diorio in the top crew?"

"Yeah, second in command, but not an enforcer."

"Figures. He had a small frame and delicate hands. He was moderately handsome. As per his landlord, he had quite a few lady friends."

"That's where his nickname came from," Antonio said. 'He favored quantity over commitment. They described him as a "Taco Juggler". Flash was his operating technique. His assignations were of the short one-night stand variety.'

"I guess we'll find out more about Mr. Frank's good and bad sides tomorrow. See you then."

Antonio, in his usual gruff style, hung up without a goodbye.

I had ingredients to buy. I was planning a nice home-cooked supper for Pat. She was now a full-time university law student. After months of work to nail fraudsters and wasted days in court, she had her fill of frustrations when seeing criminals slide by the justice system because of some small legal technicalities and, more often, because of mediocre performances from prosecuting attorneys.

"They may know book law, but they have no street experience, no knowledge of how scammers and cheats disrupt lives and harm innocent victims," Pat had said. "I'd know how to question the gurriers. I'd be deadly, a sure better job than many o'them."

When she told me she was considering a law career. I was convinced that yes, she could question troublemakers and criminal rascals better than someone with no street experience. I had fully committed to backing her up.

* * *

When I walked into the living room, Crackers, my crazy Maine-Coon, was sitting on Pat's lap, pawing at her book as she was trying to read.

"Your man is just in time. Our furry pest is complaining about his empty bowl," she said. "He's been a mischief all day."

I gave her a fast kiss on the forehead and made a grab for the cat. I wasn't fast enough. He jumped into my shopping bag, stole a package of French chicken liver paté and ran off into the kitchen.

"He's in one of his moods, isn't he?"

"I'm afeard so. I'm scarlet for forgetting to lock your office door. I tried to replant the fern, but I think it's done for."

"Not to worry, I'm surprised it lasted this long. It seems to be his nemesis. You hungry now, or do we have a later supper?"

She gave me a suggestive smile.

"A glass of wine, a hug and cuddle would be nice as openers."

I made it to the kitchen just in time to see my fluffy tailed fiend hack up a piece of wrapping from his stolen plunder. I grabbed the punctured cello pack off the floor and sliced off a corner. I filled his bowl with his favorite smelly fish mix, added the triangle of paté on top and put it in his cat corner. All of this, while he was trying to climb my right leg. Crackers, gave the paté a few licks, went to the patio door, and knocked his head against it. Cat language for let me out. There seems to be no logic to a cat's mind.

I uncorked a bottle of an Austrian Pinot Noir. Filled two glasses and headed back to the living room.

We had a late, late supper. I deduced that after being alone and reading boring law books all day, Pat had missed me.

FIVE

I'm always early for meetings. I'm not sure if this is a character quality or fault. It has, however, more than once saved me from an ambush.

Antonio had given me a key to the gym a few years back when I saved his life during one of my "off the reservation" adventures. He had since saved mine. He was up by two, but who's counting.

The alarm system was off, a potential sign that he was already in the building. I padded softly to his office behind the reception desk.

His deep voice came over the sound system.

"Stop sneaking around. You forgot about the camera at the entrance."

I opened the office door and peeked in.

"Just making sure it was you," I said. "Not some intruder."

"Did you see a dead body anywhere?"

"No."

"Then there was no intruder."

My smart-ass friend had a hot double-walled clear glass mug of coffee waiting for me on the corner of his antique desk. He pointed to it.

I took a sip.

"Your coffee has an added flavor," I said.

"Wake up your brain cells before our friend Diesel gets here," Antonio said.

"Diesel?"

"His name is Vincent, and he looks a lot like Vin Diesel."

The doorbell chimed as he finished his sentence. Antonio glanced at his monitor and pressed a button somewhere under his desk to buzz our visitor in.

Antonio was correct in his description. Vincent's shaved head was about two inches higher than mine. It put him at five-eleven or six feet even. I looked him straight in the eyes. He took off his dark glasses and I did the same. I had wider shoulders and bigger arms than he did. We both restrained ourselves from too strong a handshake.

Antonio plunked another mug of coffee on the desk.

"If you guys are finished with the macho shit, let's sit down and talk."

There was no formal introduction. Diesel took a seat and grabbed the offered coffee. He looked at me over the rim of his cup.

"You found Flash?"

"Yes, I'm sorry to say. His body was in the trunk of a rented car at Pierre Elliot Trudeau Airport. He was killed elsewhere. His throat was slit. He bled out next to his burned-out bike in a swampland north of the airport. You can be at ease. I'm in homicide, not interested in any other business he may have been up to."

"You have street cred, or I wouldn't be here," Diesel said. He took a gulp of his coffee, pursed his lips, and nodded a yes to Antonio. I guess the added booze had just hit his taste buds.

"Why was he on a dead-end marshland road late Tuesday night?" I said.

"Haven't a fuck'n clue. We had a meeting with some—business associates at a bar on Saturday night. He never showed, didn't answer his phones. It was weird. He's—was, very organized, not his style. He was always on time, to the second."

"Phones?"

"He had a few, personal, business and maybe two more. Find any on him?" Diesel said.

I shook my head.

"If the cops do. Any chance of getting them back?"

"May I ask why?"

"He had contacts I'd prefer stay private."

"By now, the lab boys have finished with the crime scene," I said. "I'll find out about the phones. If they're bagged as evidence, you'll have to write them off."

Antonio jumped into the conversation

"Slit throat, and the body moved to a relatively public place to find it. It has the feel of a hit with a message."

Diesel had a scowl on his face when he said,

"There's nothing on my radar, and certainly nothing that would warrant offing our vice president. If I had a clue, we'd be out on the street hunting. I got fuck all."

Diesel said all the right words but didn't appear overly perturbed or much sorrowed at the violent demise of his second in command.

"Nothing else?" I said.

"No, we're asking around. If I get something that we don't want to handle, I'll call." He thumb-pointed to Antonio and stood to leave.

I stayed sitting. After Diesel left, I spoke to Antonio.

"You're in the loop, as requested, my friend. It'll be your turn to inform me if he calls."

"You back on the job?"

"No, I'm here. I'll do a gym session,"

SIX

Following my workout, my plan was to head to the office and check with Dobson to see what both he and the Mrs. Lakatos team at the airport had for me. I was curious as to why Diorio had three or more phones. Hopefully, I'd get more than my meeting with Diesel. On the useful information scale, it had gained me zilch.

* * *

I sat on a low chair, the top of the lab counter at my chest level. Dobson, now dressed in his favorite pale blue rumpled lab coat perched on a stool. Doctor Jekyll type coiled glass tubes, bottles, beakers, and test tubes surrounded us.

"If you cleaned up all the reports, nasty photographs of body parts, and piles of paperwork from your office, we could sit down for a comfortable discussion, over a desk." I said.

"I-I'll get to it. We're understaffed, and—and overworked."

"You've been saying this for two years, Tristan."

Dobson shrugged.

"Still true."

I pulled out my phone and swiped to my recording software.

"I need all the details from your Diorio analysis,"

"We found a few footprints around the site. I had to reconstruct whole prints from a bunch of sloppy par-partials. From Anna I got Diorio at size US 8, 'B', forty-one European. His and another set of western boots at size US eight and a half, also 'B' width."

"It looks like only the victim and one other guy at the kill site," I said.

"Maybe another guy."

"Maybe?"

"Western boots are tricky. Could also be size ten and a half wide women's western boots."

"Tristan, why would you possibly think a woman may have killed him?"

"Weapon was extremely li-like a Japanese kitchen paring or boning knife. No bruises or trauma marks on the body. Men generally dominate the victim with holds and punches."

"I'm leaning toward a professional hitter on a fast job that would not leave evidence," I said. "No marks, no bullet to match to a gun. Had to be strong to carry a dead body all the way back to the road and dump it in a car trunk,"

"Also, a plausible theory," Dobson said.

"Did you find a cell phone at the site?"

"Two burned up in the bike sa,saddle bags. Part of another, smashed on rocks between the kill zone and the road."

"Can you get any info at all from the broken phone?"

"No, but Anna found a small flip model hidden in his jacket sleeve."

"Will you be able to see what's on that phone?"

He reached into his lab coat and handed me a little black plastic USB key.

"Done."

I was about to tell him I loved him when my phone interrupted my errant thought. O'Neil's number was on the screen. Once more, my boss's secret power found me before I could sneak out of headquarters. Annoyed, I swiped open the green phone icon.

"Beaudry, talk to me."

"Lieutenant Beaudry, could you please join me in the fourth-floor boardroom. I have guests waiting to meet you."

"Be there in five," I said.

"Fine, we'll be expecting you shortly."

This strangely polite call did not fit O'Neil's normal curt phone behavior. What the heck was this all about?

SEVEN

It perturbed me when I walked into the boardroom and saw everyone in formal attire. My mind fast registered insignias, gold stripes on sleeves, ribbons, and medals on uniforms. For an uneasy moment, it rang of military court martial. I've earned a reputation for getting into gun fights with bad guys, and I've lost several pages from the police procedures manual over the years. It has simplified my work on the street and gave me the flexibility to earn top position for the best case solved ratio, ever. My worry dissipated. I realized that there was no representative from Internal Affairs in the room.

My boss was on one side of the wide table next to the assistant director. Two tough-looking high-ranking officers from Sureté du Québec, our provincial police service, were across from them.

O'Neil pointed to the high back-office chair at the end of the table. I guessed that this was the designated hot seat.

I dumped my rear onto the fancy chair and addressed my boss.

"Your meeting," I said.

He nodded to the provincial officers.

"Actually, it's their meeting,"

I pulled out my note pad and O'Neil shook his finger at me in a "No" motion.

He introduced both SQ officers with their official French titles. Thirty seconds later, I had forgotten their names.

One was a DGA, a Deputy Director in the criminal investigations division, the other a Chief Inspector in the same division.

The Chief inspector was the spokesperson. On both sides, the top brass were observers only. Probably to make sure that the

27

complicated politics of inter-agency cooperation would be deemed to be observed.

"Lieutenant Beaudry, you have a reputation for—action and lone wolf tactics. We don't want to interfere with your murder investigation."

I interrupted his holier-than-thou speech.

"I work several cases at a time. Which one are you referring to?"

"The biker found yesterday at the Trudeau airport. We have an active investigation with these same bikers that we'd not appreciate interference with."

I put my hands palm out at shoulder height, in I give up symbol.

"I wouldn't dream of compromising another investigation. What makes you worry about this?"

"You met with Vincent Gilbert, the biker's president, early this morning at a health club."

"Ah, the tan Subaru Impreza that followed me for six blocks before I lost him. I figured it was a member of the gang. Not an SQ tail. Else, I would have stopped and had a coffee with them."

My comment got a flat mustache smile from O'Neil, wide eyes from our assistant director, and puckered lips from the other side of the table.

"My murder case has elements of a professional hit with a message. I wanted to find out if there was another biker war in the works. If I knew more about your investigation, I'd make sure not to muddy the waters on your side."

The SQ inspector looked at his boss, who gave him an inconspicuous nod.

"We believe there is a new Far East drug importer operating in Montreal and in provinces out west," he said. "Rumors have it that the bikers are trying to get distribution rights. That's all I can tell you for the moment."

"Thanks for the heads up on that. It could easily create a conflict with the cartel suppliers and with rival distributors. The biker president may have blatantly lied to me this morning. Diorio's murder as a second in command looks more and more like an organized hit and a message sent to the club. By the way, his name on the street is Diesel, because he looks like the movie star Vin Diesel."

To my great surprise, our Assistant Director backed me up with a subtle final comment.

"We all agree that murder one trumps drug distribution. I'm sure that Lieutenant Beaudry will have his lips sealed about your investigation and keep you informed on anything that may help you. Gentlemen, I think we'll end this meeting. I'll accompany you for lunch in our cafeteria if you please.

I begged off. I had other plans for my day.

EIGHT

I called Sergeant Nico DiLalla from the anti-gang squad. I'd been friends with Nico since our academy days together. He was a good cop and should have been promoted a long time ago. That in his large Italian family he had cousins on the other side of the badge didn't help his image with our politically sensitive brass.

"Sorry to disturb. You free for a late lunch?"

"I'm just finishing an interview uptown close to the Greek seafood place on Decarie, *magari* another fifteen minutes."

"Your maybe fifteen minutes is okay. I'll meet you there."

"*Va bene, ci vediamo.*"

I hung with Nico enough to understand eighty percent of his Italian. On the other hand, he says I still speak it like a Spanish cow.

I pressed the elevator button for the ground floor and to our parking at the rear of the building.

* * *

There were the usual orange cone diversions and barriers along the construction projects downtown. I made it to the restaurant in thirty-eight minutes, not fifteen.

Nico was at a table in the rear of the place, chatting with the chef. Once more, dressed as if he had just left a men's fashion magazine shoot. As if he was a movie star, he always wore the current in-fashion clothes. In the drug an street gang world, he could get away with it. He blended in well with the wealthy and similarly fancy dressed distributors.

Today, it looked like a cotton-silk sports jacket in delicate tones of gray and soft pink. Undoubtedly, from some famous Italian designer. I thought the bright blue floppy handkerchief draped out of his breast pocket was overkill. But then I'm not much of a fashionista.

Trying my best not to look like a cop. I'm more discreet. I favor jeans, a sober T-shirt sans advertising, or a sports shirt and a blazer worn only to conceal my Miami shoulder rig and weapon.

As I approached the table, the chef went back to work.

"You exchanging recipes?"

"No, just inquiring about his family. Contrary to you, Carmen takes care of the kitchen and all the cooking," Nico said.

"Pat now does a little puttering in the kitchen," I said. "I do most of it because I love to cook. In my teen years, when I lived on the farm with my dad and uncle, we would take turns at preparing the meals, each trying to outdo the others. I got good at it."

"Speaking of cooking," Nico said. "What's this meeting about, something on the back burner or boiling over on the stove?"

"A bit of both. I'm on the murder of the number two man in a biker gang. His throat was slit, and the body dumped in the trunk of a car at the airport. I had a sit-down with the gang's leader, Diesel. He seemed little disturbed by the lack of a second in command. I was leaning to an internal reorganization and going along my merry little way until I was called to an unusual meeting this morning. It included our SPVM brass and some multi-striped SQ department heads. They told me not to step on their narco investigation of the same gang. I figured if drugs were involved, you would know about it."

"Diesel's gang?"

"Ya, our victim is V.P. Frank Diorio, nicknamed Flash. I'll text you his driver's permit. You'll have his mug to show if you talk to anyone. I don't have much so far. I appreciate any help. Diesel told me point-blank he has fuck all on the murder. If he had, they'd be on the war path. Not sure how truthful he was."

"Ah, *capisco. Primo,* Diesel, got to be head of the gang by cheating, bullying and mostly by outright lying and truth bending."

"He gave me the impression of sneaky politician," I said.

"*É vero. Secundo,* the provincial police, is always ten feet behind the soccer ball. They're not regulars on the street. I know the bikers are currently negotiating the distribution rights with a new Vietnamese importer on the scene. My informers tell me that Eastland Hardware and Electric, a company with offices in Montreal, Toronto and somewhere else in a western province, are running a side-line product. The name Tràn Van Bào, one of the company owners, keeps popping up in conversations about snow or nose candy."

The waiter came to give us the menu. I told him we'd give him a sign.

"So, to make a bad pun, Diesel snowed me. It's beginning to look more and more like an internal hit, maybe by an outside pro, to make sure everybody in the gang has an alibi," I said.

"If it was a pro, good luck on that. He's done his job and flown away," Nico said.

"On the flip side of the coin," I said. "The only aggrieved people in this scenario would be the South American cartel currently distributing the flake. That may warrant a warning about changing to another supplier."

"*Pero,* a clean slice doesn't look like the type of message the Mexicans normally send. The new Jalisco cartel is hanging mutilated bodies from overpass bridges on the other side of the U.S. border as a warning to rival gangs. That's today's style."

"You may be right. We've had one murder in the North of town," I said. "Victim and car riddled with military rifle caliber rounds. AK forty-seven machine gun style on full auto. Plus, in the past three weeks, we had two missed attempts where the victim survived. It may not yet be a war, but it's an unmistakable warning for someone."

"I'll keep my eyes and ears open for info on your guy," Nico said.

It was past one, and the restaurant had near emptied. Our waiter was patiently hovering in the background. I didn't want to overtax his patience. I motioned him over.

I went for the swordfish steak, Nico, the grilled shrimp.

We hadn't seen each other for months. We forgot business and chatted about family and sports.

Both Nico and I skipped the honeyed Greek desserts. He promised to get more info on Diesel's business dealings and keep me informed. It was past three when I took care of the bill.

NINE

My job isn't like the usual television portrayals of detectives. I don't solve a single case in an hour less the commercials. Even the slam dunk ones where the perpetrator is found at the scene with a gun in his hand.

It takes weeks and most often months or years to clear a murder case and bring it to prosecution. I'm always working on several murders at the same time.

After my meeting with the SQ cops, I had called Dobson asking him to feed me details of his forensic analysis as soon as he got anything new. I was likewise waiting for Antonio and now Nico to get back to me with more news from their on-the-street informants.

A 'call me 911' text message from Dobson popped in as soon as I closed my car door. The 911 showed it was urgent. I responded before starting my Jeep and braving the end of day traffic.

His number is second after Pat on my favorite list.

He answered on the first ring.

"I, I found a g-ghost."

"Whoa horsey, take a deep breath, slow down Tristan."

For a few seconds, I heard heavy breathing.

"I found—a long female i-red hair on a cattail at the biker site."

"I'm sure that Pat has a good alibi," I said.

"Listen, listen. On, on a whim, I checked it against last springtime's Jane Doe redhead. The DNA ma, matches."

"What, are you serious?"

I'm working on a year-old case that another homicide team asked for my help on. The naked body of a thirtyish, pretty redhead had been discovered in a dumpster at the rear of an up-town restaurant. Her fingerprints were not on file, and we didn't have a missing person report opened, nor any to this date. The only distinguishing mark was the tattoo of a bird with multicolored wings on her forearm. We had classed her as an unknown Jane Doe.

The restaurant owner who found her was in tears when the original detectives interviewed him. He had to be hospitalized for psychological trauma. The story had hit the front pages, and he opted to close his restaurant due to all the adverse publicity and false rumors about the cleanliness of his kitchen. It put an abrupt, unfortunate end to his restaurant career.

Dobson's team had determined the Jane Doe victim had traces of the date-rape drug Rohypnol in her blood. She had in fact been raped, then strangled during, or immediately after. There had been a trace of unknown DNA in her vagina. It was evidence from her aggressor, but we had nothing to compare it with.

"The hair was there since last year?" I said. "Don't tell me they murdered her at the same site, then dumped the body uptown."

"No, no, the elements did not deteriorate the hair. Be, besides cattails go dormant in winter, they decay and sprout back. This was a fresh hair on fresh growth."

"You're telling me that the dead girl, or her ghost, was at the biker kill site at the same time as Diorio?"

"No, I was joking about a, a ghost. I'm telling you that her hair was. Someone was in contact a year ago with Jane Doe. Some of her hair got on his clothes and he wore the same jacket this spring to the current crime scene."

"So it may be the same killer. We might solve two crimes in one fell swoop," I said.

"Emphasis on, on the might," Dobson said.

"Oh ye of little faith," I said. "Call me back if you have anything else. Weird or not. And can you send me a picture of your ghost redhead to remind me?"

My years on the job taught me there aren't meaningless concurrences. Every coincidence signals a clue that needs further analysis.

That bit of information also put a different twist on my assumptions. It was now doubtful that a Mexican cartel killer was involved. This new discovery swung the needle of my theory compass to a local killer, and the possibility of an internal reorganization of the biker gang.

I left a message for Antonio asking him to set up another meet with Diesel. Maybe this time he'd slip up on the bullshit he shoveled at me the last time.

I had not yet checked the USB key Dobson gave me. I saved it for Pat. Her skill in computers, plus the years she worked in the fraud squad, had earned her the reputation of the best "white hat hacker" in the department. I was eager for her to find more clues from Diorio's phone records.

TEN

I arrived home earlier than usual. I opened the front door to the whirring sound of a vacuum cleaner. We had discussed hiring a housekeeper last week, when my black and white crazy cat showed up for supper dragging a large dust bunny from the end of his tail. We took turns at keeping everything tidy, but Pat was busy with law courses. Her sessions were mornings, afternoons, and occasionally evenings. In my job, a work schedule didn't exist. They could pull in me at any hour of any day of the week or weekend.

The person maneuvering our seldom used dust gobbling, egg-shaped Sebo was a strong-looking middle-aged, short-haired auburn lady with perfect facial skin. She stomped the machine off and gave me a big smile.

"Your lady is in the washroom trying to console the cat," she said.

I extended my hand to her.

"Robert," I said.

With a firm grip and the same big smile, she answered, "Neda."

She tapped the machine on and returned to her cleaning. I headed to the washroom to question my favorite redhead on this fresh development.

Pat and Crackers were cuddling on the floor of my double-sized shower. My furry fiend wrapped in one of my large bath towels. Only his head was visible. His ears pulled back against his head, eyes wide, and wild looking, he didn't look like a happy camper.

"We've found the Achilles' heel of your cat here. He's deadly afeared of the vac," Pat said.

"I think that mother cats tell their kittens a story about a noisy machine that once sucked the tail right off a cat. It's their boogie man," I said.

"I had to wrap him in your man's towel. He was trying to claw my hand off, in a panic he was."

I dropped to one knee. Crackers seemed to calm down upon seeing me.

"Neda?"

"An opportunity that was. When I came home from class, she was standing sad and forlorn in front of the house across the street."

"The one where Mr. James, the engineer guy with the big beard, lived?"

"Ah, right. She's been keeping it clean ever since he passed away, she has. Once a month. Today was her day. Mr. James's *bowsie* son put the place up for sale this morning without even tellin, her."

"So we lucked out."

Pat gave me a wink. She stood up, and I took the cat bundle.

"Tell Nida to hold off on the vacuuming for a couple of minutes. I'll put Crackers out till supper."

* * *

I had done no shopping today. I managed a vegetarian pizza with some flatbread that I had frozen last week, varied color peppers, onions, tomatoes, and some fresh basil. A Spanish Jumilla wine paired well.

Neda had left, but Crackers refused to come into the house. I filled his bowl with his fishy favorite wet food and left it outside. He'd finish his pouting, eventually.

During supper, I brought Pat up to date on my current case.

"I need a favor," I said.

"Does that have anything to do with a bedroom?"

"I have a USB with phone records from the victim. I need a computer expert to find the names and addresses of his last week's calls."

"Well, that's a disappointment, it is," Pat said with a lascivious grin.

"Of course I'd expect to pay a bonus for the overtime work," I said.

"Fierce, I'll start while you clean up."

By the time I cleaned up the supper dishes and let Crackers in, Pat had finished the search.

Diorio had thirteen calls on his phone the week before his murder. She got all thirteen names and addresses for me to follow up.

We drifted to the bedroom, and I made good on my promise of a bonus.

ELEVEN

After breakfast, Pat sped away to an early class, and I spent a difficult twenty minutes outside on the balcony, trying to comb out a couple of fur knots above Cracker's tailbone. This time, I took the precaution of wearing work gloves. There was no loss of blood on my part, and no animals were hurt in the process. It was, however, a serious contortionist challenge to hold my squirming and hissing monster with one hand, and the FURminator untangling comb with the other.

My breathing was back to normal when I arrived at the gym a half hour after opening. I planned to do a short work out, then start on the list Pat had printed for me. All the calls were from, or to, women. The phone Dobson's team found must be devoted to his rendezvous dating.

As I finished my last bench press rep, Antonio surprised me. From my supine position, I saw him upside down behind me. He walked off after a curt reminder.

"Come see me when you're finished cleaning up your equipment."

An aggravating habit on his part. I had never used equipment without wiping it up and putting it back where it was supposed to be. That was one lesson I learned in my youth from my uncle Bruno, the mechanic and expert woodworker. Tools cleaned and back in the cabinet was his standing rule.

* * *

When I stepped into his office, Antonio had a fresh cup of coffee waiting for me.

"It's hot. Your timing is always right," I said.

He swiveled the monitor on his desk to my side. He had the screen split into views from four different cameras. One was the exit of the dressing room.

"You shouldn't have shown me your secret." I said. "It's always a downer when you find out how the magician does the trick."

Never one to waste words, he said,

"Meeting with Diesel. Ten p.m. Uptown at Sharky's pool bar."

"We?"

"Your meeting. I'm your backup. I've got bad vibes about this one."

Antonio saved my life more than once. I didn't question his esoteric comment. While I drank my coffee, I told him about my case and my suspicions. The update ended with my last sip.

"Go to the meeting. I'll be somewhere in the shadows," he said.

"You are a shadow," I said. "On that subject, I had a car tailing me last Thursday. I thought it was one of Diesel's people. It turned out it was the SQ. They were sloppy, and I lost them easily. It appears they have an eye on the gang's drug operation that they don't want me to step on."

"When you drive to the meeting, you won't see me, but I'll be somewhere behind to make sure you don't have a tail," Antonio said.

I left the gym in a rush. I had groceries to fetch and a list of things to accomplish today.

* * *

I did my shopping, restocked my larder, and prepared a supper plate for Pat. I filled Cracker's food bowl and refreshed his cat fountain with fresh water. He was still out on his usual morning hunt.

At 4:15 this morning, his moping from the vacuum cleaner incident had subsided. He serenaded us awake with howls, asking to be let back in.

I changed clothes, and in respect for Antonio's premonition, donned a Silent Partner body armor undershirt, and added a compact .380 pistol held in a small of back DeSantis holster for today's attire. I sent Pat a text telling her I'd be working late tonight. I then headed downtown to headquarters to contact the women from Pat's research. Their phone would indicate a call from the Montreal Police. I figured it would be a better attention getter than a call from an unknown person.

* * *

From my list of Diorio's thirteen women contacts from the week before his untimely death, I reached twelve. I found it curious that one number came up as no longer in service.

My score was three voice mails asking to leave a message. I did. Four that I disturbed at work. They promised to call me back. I gave out my unlisted private home number. Pat had programmed a separate line on the answering machine.

I'd have to explain to her before a gaggle of strange women called me. She has a surprisingly jealous streak that I'm flattered by. However, the color of her hair is my reminder of her Irish fiery temper that I'm always best to consider.

Two women hung up as soon as I mentioned Frank's name. Three others were keen to talk to me.

"Sandra, this is Lieutenant Robert Beaudry from the major crimes division Montreal police. I'd need to ask you a few brief questions about Frank Diorio."

"Why are you calling me?"

"Your name came up in my investigation."

"What, what do you want to know? I met him twice. That was it."

"What was your impression of him?"

"He was a real charmer when I first met him at a bar downtown. We had one other date, and he never called me back, end of story."

"Did you try to contact him?"

"No, no, I had broken off with my boyfriend and I dated a few men. I clicked with one guy and we're seeing each other. I don't want to fuck it up," she said. "What did Frank do to earn a police investigation?"

"Just part of a routine check," I said. "I appreciate your answers. Thank you very much."

The start of my questioning with the two others was basically the same. The answers, much different.

"Well, he's a sweet talker, but one of those slam bang, thank you ma'am, types that never call you back. What exactly do you want to know?" Nancy said.

"It's part of a routine investigation. I'm looking to get a better handle on his personality, and what his mindset was at the time you met him."

"He's charming, well spoken, polite, but somewhat forceful. His mind was set between my legs, and he knew what he was doing. We met on Tuesday, and he promised to call me Friday for another date and, whatever. When he didn't, it pissed me off. When I tried to call him, he had blocked my number. It would ring once and hang up. Tell him fuck you from me."

I got more from my last call. My introduction and the reason I was calling, a better handle on his personality, mindset, yada, yada, yada was the same.

"Yes, he was charming and funny. We had a great supper at a steak place. He paid the bill and was a gentleman during the meal. It was evident, though, he expected I would be dessert," Barbara said.

"He had a reputation as a—playboy. How was he with you?" I said.

"Had. Is he dead?"

"I'm afraid so. He was in a motorcycle gang. I don't know if it has anything to do with his death. That's what I'm investigating. I'd need to hear more about your meeting with him. Every little bit helps."

"I'm not surprised that he's dead. There was something dangerous about him, in his eyes. I dunno, I just felt better going to my place, not his. He wasn't much on foreplay. I pushed him back at one point and he got angry fast. I told him he could leave. It switched him back to his charming self. We had a parting shot of tequila and wound up in bed. He had moves that most men have not mastered. I must have had a bit too much to drink. I woke up the next morning in a messed-up bed with blank spots about what happened. Frank had vanished, gone, no note, nothing."

"Did you call him back, or did he call you?"

"No and no, I wouldn't have gone out with him again. Something just didn't feel right."

After we hung up, parts of her comments sent my suspicion meter ringing. She appeared ready to kick him out after a show of violence on his part, then after a last drink, they wound up rolling in the hay, and she intimated a memory lapse. It felt like a potential repeat of Dobson's reconstruction of the Jane doe murder, except no dead body, this time.

I ordered a loaded pizza and ate it at my desk while finishing some paperwork. Five minutes before I left for my meet with Diesel, my boss called to find out why I was working late, and to inquire on how my investigation was progressing. I didn't bother asking how the heck he knew I was in my office. I gave him a fast redacted version and headed out to my meeting.

The weather had changed from a hot and humid day to an overcast, sticky evening.

TWELVE

The slow traffic and detours gobbled up the twenty-minute leeway I had given myself. Montreal is a giant construction project. Why the powers that be decided to repair and or modernize the city's roads and infrastructure all at once was beyond logic and comprehension. Mind you, that seems the norm for any government decision these days. They had closed the 136 downtown beltway again. I relied on the GPS lady to get me out of the orange coned mess I was in.

Traffic thinned when I swung onto the belowground Decarie Boulevard. The route North stayed clear up to Sharky's bar. But the weather didn't. The afternoon overcast had morphed into murky low hanging cumulus clouds. I saw a few flashes of lightning on the western horizon.

* * *

I walked into the bar. The lighting was dimmed, the corners dark, it didn't create a romantic atmosphere, like the weather, it leaned more to ominous.

I scanned the room for exits and potential traps. A habit acquired over the years of police work on the street. There were four full patched bikers perched on backless stools at the bar. Diesel's shiny head was the farthest from the door and my entrance. The bartender was a tall, full, rounded, over-make-upped bottle blonde with shoulder length, very curly hair. She wore an abundantly filled red halter top and tight fitted white summer jeans. I'd have to ask Pat how women accomplished those wide, frizzy stand-up hairstyles. Maybe it has something to do with a jolt of electricity.

Somebody sitting at the bar commented,

"The cop's on time."

I replied, "If you've been told that you are late and unreliable more than once, not only do you lack punctuality, but you also lack decency and seriousness, which makes you contemptuous."

Diesel stood up and motioned me to the stool next to him.

"Time for a game," he said to his followers.

From an under counter switch, the bar lady turned on the overhead lights for the billiard area.

The three leather jacket guys headed for the tables at the far end of the room.

"I was told you talk fancy shit," Diesel said. "What was that quote?"

"It's my interpretation of what some Indian guru whose name I don't remember said."

I nodded toward the frizzy-haired blonde.

"Speaking of talking shit, you okay talking business here?"

Diesel smiled at her.

"Sophia's my old lady. We have an understanding."

She pulled out a fine gold chain from the cleft between her bosoms. There was a gold band dangling from the end. Her voice was soft and melodious.

"What do you want to drink, Lieutenant?"

I looked at the logos on the handles of the on-tap beers.

"Ricard's Red is fine."

Diesel nodded. She poured two mugs.

We both had a first sip before speaking.

"It's come to my attention that you're negotiating with Tràn Van Bào for the distribution rights of one of his Vietnamese imported products," I said. "Would Frank's death be a consequence of that transaction? An unhappy current supplier, perhaps?"

I had expected my information to surprise Diesel. He only gave me a bland look. When he spoke, I was the surprised one.

"Your information's out of date," he said. "That business finished over six weeks ago. We're expanding our sales east and north of Quebec. We'll probably buy the same quantity from our current suppliers. There should be no hard feelings."

"Well, that crosses off that lead," I said.

"I guess you're not the only cop to have this info," Diesel said.

In retrospect, it was childish of me to want to get back at the arrogance of the SQ at yesterday's meeting. I hadn't liked their attitude at all. I may not follow procedures to the letter, but I get the job done. I was out on a limb, a skinny shaky unstable one.

"Like I told you, I'm homicide. Recreational pharmacology is not my area of worry. In fact, as of now, nobody in the SPVM seems much interested in your dealings."

Diesel pulled at my branch.

"Not Montreal Police?"

I was now on a meager twig over the fire pit of disloyalty. I shrugged. It was up to him to read between the lines.

I stayed mute, looked away, and studied the effervescent brew in my mug.

He took a couple of swigs of beer before changing the subject.

"Frank traded up his bike for a new Harley last summer. He's had an elaborate paint job done since and added a lot of artistic custom work at three different shops. He had the fanciest wheels in town. It must have cost him a bundle. He was our treasurer. Instead of worrying about where he found the cash, I had our accountant check the books. All was in order on our side. He was a smart-ass, fast to use his fists. He may have shafted somebody in a deal that has nothing to do with the club, disrespected or pushed a man he shouldn't have."

"The fancy work he had done is interesting. I was thinking of looking for a custom shop in town to jazz up my Jeep," I said.

Diesel made a writing motion on the bar top. Sophia fished out a pen from under the counter. He scribbled the names of three businesses on his bar coaster and slid it my way. I guess he could now say with honesty that he never *spoke* to me about them.

We finished another mug with small talk. I found out that Diesel and Sophia had been a couple for the last seventeen years, and that they had a teenage daughter currently in rebel mode.

I didn't comment or offer my condolences.

Our friendly chat was suddenly interrupted. We heard the wind-driven pelting rain lash at the windows. It was loud enough to drown out the sound of the clicking pool balls from the players on the other side of the room. The clouds had suddenly dumped their load of acid rain on Montreal Island.

THIRTEEN

The expression raining buckets, I can understand. The raining cats and dogs one is a puzzle. I hesitated a few minutes in the darkened vestibule. I looked through the glass front door, hoping for a break in the downpour.

I didn't get one. The weather gods had voted for a steady drenching, combined with a few fireworks. Lightning illuminated the sky to my right, showing me the outline of two men sitting in a Cadillac SUV two cars next to mine. They were staring in my direction. The roar of thunder came after several seconds. The bolt of lightning had struck miles away. On the other side of my measurement, the goons in the Caddy felt way too close, and certainly more dangerous to me than the distant lighting.

I'm uncertain if Antonio's premonition, or the prospect of cold rain dripping into my collar, caused it, but I felt a sudden chill rush down my backbone. I slid my gun out of my shoulder holster and held it hidden down by my leg. I flung open the door and quick marched to my Jeep. I had my empty hand up, ready to reach for my door handle when I felt a jab in my left side.

A short stocky man in a black hooded rain poncho had a sawed-off shotgun jabbed into my ribs. He put his left hand out, his fingers signaled me in an open and closing motion.

"Gun," he said, "slow and easy."

It's a known fact learned too late by many a dead man, that you can't outdraw a pointed gun. In slow motion, I raised my weapon to the front. Holding the grip by my thumb and forefinger, I let the barrel twist down, pointing to the ground. I didn't give it to him. I dropped it next to my car. At the metallic clunk, he glanced down. In that second, his attention drifted away from me. I twisted aside, batting his shotgun barrel to my left and simultaneously, I snatched out my hidden compact gun. I pulled the trigger twice while I was still moving it upward. My second shot must have gone under his chin straight up into his brain stem, his body functions switched to off. His eyes rolled back, and he followed in that direction, slumping to the ground with a splash. Another fateful lightning strike showed me the two men from the Cadillac were now on the other side of my Jeep. They both had sawed-off shotguns.

The first guy poked his weapon around the rear of my Jeep. Before he could level it, I heard the metallic snap and muted cough of a suppressed weapon repeated several times in rapid succession.

My aggressor dropped to the pavement face first. A thin pink stream of blood mixing with the rain dripped from his forehead. The second man was moaning from somewhere behind him.

I heard Antonio before I saw him come out from the dark.

"You okay Robert?"

"Yeah, your premonition helped. It primed me for action before the first guy attacked. I guess you're up for another lifesaving medal," I said.

"In reality, I stopped *two* guys that were gunning for you, but who's counting."

The front door of the club flung open. The bikers ran toward us with guns in hand. Diesel was in the lead and the first one to speak.

"We heard gunshots. What the fuck is this?"

"Somebody planned an ambush. Lucky for me I had back-up," I said.

Antonio, dressed in imitation black swat team attire, had his rifle cradled in his arms and a nasty scowl on his face. Diesel looked his way and shook his head. "Nothing to do with us."

The bikers were fast to snatch up the weapons strewn on the ground. In my adrenaline high, I laughed when one of them said,

They all have the same type of twelve gauge. There must have been a sale.

Another biker stood over the still alive and moaning guy.

"I recognize him. He works for Santino."

Diesel tucked his revolver into his belt.

"Your comment of an unhappy supplier may have merit," he said. "With all due respect, Lieutenant, we don't want cops in our front yard. Get the fuck away from here. We'll take care of this mess." He nodded to the Santino shooter, "Hang on buddy, we'll get you patched up, but first I have a few questions."

"I have no problem with you cleaning up," I said. "I hate paperwork, and more so Internal Affairs. Make it fast. The rain is ruining your leather jackets."

"We'll send you the bill," Diesel said.

Antonio handed him the night vision scoped and custom outfitted AR15.

"Here's a deposit," he said.

I opened my car door, took out a window rag from the console, wiped my small backup gun and handed it over. Diesel inherited all the evidence. I took my dropped pistol from the ground, put it in my pocket and said to Antonio,

"Gym tomorrow morning. I'll text you."

FOURTEEN

On the road home, my sodden clothes stuck uncomfortably to my body, aggravating an already foul mood. Firstly, I hate guns pointed at me. Secondly, I was worried that the muffed attack could be the start of another gang war. I was also uneasy owing a debt to Diesel and Company for cleaning up my mess.

I arrived just past one a.m. Pat had left the reading lamp next to the living room armchair on as a night light for me. I slipped off my damp shoes and padded to the bathroom to drape my waterlogged clothes on the shower's glass side. Pat had left a stack of fresh towels in my bathroom. When we moved in together, we did some major renovations that included separate his and hers bathrooms. Even with both of our crazy schedules, we have no conflict. She has a nice perfume scent to her bathroom. None of that I just came back from a tough gym workout man scent or the random mishap from Crackers who occasionally uses my shower drain instead of his litter box. On my side, I no longer have lacy things hung here, there, and everywhere, nor countless gold or silver-trimmed jars, multiple boxes of cotton balls and expensive tubes of "I don't know what", encircling my sink.

I wiped myself dry, then returned most of the two mugs of beer I had rented.

I slipped into bed without waking Pat. Crackers cuddled next to her, upside down in a semicircle. For a second, he blinked open one eye and promptly went back to cat dreamland.

At four twenty a.m. I woke from a dream. I had put huge weights on a barbell, and unable to lift it, I was being crushed. I opened my eyes to Crackers spread eagle on my chest, sniffing my beer breath. I took it as a hint that it was time for him to go out on a morning hunt.

When I got back to bed, Pat was propped up on her pillow.

"Did you just get in?"

"No, I came to bed around one. Both you and Crackers were fast asleep. Thanks for the towels and leaving a light on."

"It was lashing out. I figured you'd get caught in the storm."

"You're an angel. I'd kiss you all over."

"Can your man wait till *mornin*? I need my beauty sleep." She gave me a pat on the bum, rolled over, sighed, and immediately went into the slow breathing rhythm of sleep.

* * *

We had a relaxing weekend breakfast.

I was up and about twenty minutes before Pat dragged herself out of bed and made it to the breakfast nook.

Her hair was sleep mussed up, and she wore one of my short-sleeved Orvis check shirts three sizes too large for her, over pale blue panties. She looked like a model for a French perfume ad. I was seriously regretting that I got up before her.

She drizzled a dab of light maple syrup on her waffle.

"Low cal, non-gluten blueberry this morning. You can have two if you want. They won't break your calorie meter," I said.

Pat shook her head "no".

"Your man has messages on the machine from a couple of ladies wanting you to call them back."

I started to say, "I can explain—."

She pointed her fork at me.

"You big buffoon. I'm not daft. I recognize the names from the list I made you yesterday. You look *bolloxed up* this *mornin.*"

"This case is a mind-boggling challenge. I've got plenty of clues, but each one sends me in a different direction. I'm in a holding pattern, circling the airport, but I can't land. I have but one solid fact, victim Frank Diorio was not loved and admired by many. A gigolo, a smooth-talking liar who turned violent at the least provocation. Even his boss, the gang leader, didn't trust him a hundred percent. The list of potential haters is stretching every day."

"By the by, I'm after telling you, for women, trust is not a percentage thingy. It's an off or on switch. You trust or you absolutely don't."

"No argument, madam's philosophy is correct," I said. "That's what stumps me. Who on my long and varied list had enough to lose that it was worth killing Diorio?"

"Speaking of long and varied," Pat said. "I've pages and pages of case studies to review. I'm stuck at reading all weekend. Mind you, the weather's still manky. It's not much loss."

"Another exam next week?" I said.

"It's a class I'm *douin* well at. I've been steady in the top five. Now in the last test, I was in the top three," she said.

"Wow, great. Rain or not, we'll go have a nice supper at Antonio's bistro. We should celebrate your efforts."

"You're sweeter than this syrup," Pat said.

"Let's put it to the test," I said.

I dabbed a drop of the maple spread on my lips and kissed her on the mouth.

One thing led to another. Besides, last night I had promised to kiss her all over.

* * *

Later that morning, I phoned the women that had left messages. In different voices and levels of anger, they confirmed what I already knew. Frank was a skirt-chasing rat with a skillful tail. I didn't, however, see that as a powerful motive for his murder. Mind you, the adage that there is no fury greater than that of a scorned woman may yet prove me wrong.

Saturday and Sunday were my days of rest from my weight training regimen. I texted Antonio that I'd be at the gym for a debrief with him just before lunch. I hoped he'd take the hint.

When I left to meet him, I gave Pat a fast goodbye kiss. She was curled up on the living room sofa reading a thick leather-bound book, a bedroom pillow placed strategically behind her. She was visibly settled in for the long term.

Crackers was dangling on his side over the pile of books next to her. How a cat can sleep peacefully in such a contorted position is a feline physical enigma.

This morning, he had refused to go out in the morning drizzle. Instead, he opted for his seldom used litter box in my washroom. Myself, I braved the elements in my old trusty Burberry raincoat and a vintage Expo's baseball cap.

FIFTEEN

Antonio is quick on the uptake. He understood my text requesting a meeting just before lunch. He had ordered two Gargantua pizzas. The one with meat, meat, and meat, over, under and in between the veggie and cheese toppings.

"Let's have lunch before we talk business," he said.

We did. At the end of our meal, he didn't suggest a cup of coffee. It was a tumbler of something stronger.

"This is something different. I get a spicy ginger or pepper taste that smooths out for a soft fruity finish. I'd guess this is from your expensive reserve," I said. "Are you trying to soften the blow for some bad news?"

"Just trying to perk up a gray miserable day. Besides, we're celebrating that we're both with no holes or wounds this morning. It could have gone badly last night," Antonio said.

"I wore a level IIIA soft body armor," I said.

"Been there, done that," Antonio said. "The vest is bullet resistant, but not hurt resistant. I was nailed once from a twelve gauge at close range. The buckshot felt like a strike from a sledge hammer. It paralyzed me. If I hadn't fired in reflex as I was falling, he would have finished me. I had a bruise the size of a watermelon across my chest. It was painful for weeks."

"I've heard worse stories. Vests are not one hundred percent protection. So far, my luck has held," I said.

"And the luck is extending today," Antonio said. "There are no conflicts or potential wars on the horizon in town. Diesel paid a visit to one of his suppliers very early this morning. With twenty-something of his bikers. They came to a friendly understanding."

"With twenty mean-looking bikers around, it probably facilitated the negotiations," I said.

Before I left, we finished another tumbler of his smooth Glenrothes Speyside.

SIXTEEN

My car radio suddenly muted. The brusque tone of O'Neil's voice replaced the blues song. It was not a pleasant change.

"Beaudry, are you on a mission to antagonize the SQ?"

"Although that would be a tempting project, no. I'm not aware that I rattled their cage," I said.

"Apparently, you had another meeting at a biker's bar. Our top brass has scheduled you for a meeting with Internal Affairs on Monday morning. They want to make sure that we're politically and inter-agency correct."

"I told them straight out that I'm still investigating the murder. A lady bartender I interviewed, talked about the habits of the victim. I said. Nothing else," I lied.

"Just giving you a heads up. Give me your side of the story after the meeting. I want to make sure we're both on the same page," O'Neil said before he hung up.

If I read between the lines correctly, he was in my corner on this one.

I headed for the custom shops that Diesel had scribbled on my bar coaster. Two of the three were open on Saturday.

* * *

My first stop was MM Custom on downtown St Catherine Street. Today was the first real hint that spring was leading us to warmer weather. The sky was the pale blue of summer, and the temperature was five degrees higher than the average for the period. I chose the Decarie expressway south from Antonio's place as the fastest route. The day was so nice, and both custom stores would be open till five today. What was the rush. On a whim, I turned East at Sherbrooke Street, opting for the scenic route. I drove with my windows down and followed the slower pace of traffic past the McGill university campus. The older turn of the century architecture of Montreal blended strangely well with the glass and metal modern towers of the financial and business district. It gave a picture of yesterday and today. I passed the sober Masonic Memorial Temple and the columned Museum of Fine Arts. It was a day to enjoy being alive. I turned south at Pie IX Boulevard. With a few detours for one-way streets and a road closed for construction, I made it to the custom shop. I lucked out and found a parking spot only a few steps from the front door. I was in a good mood.

The beer-bellied ponytailed guy at the front counter had a 'Star Wars' Tee shirt and a sour look on his face.

"Good afternoon, you know Frank Diorio?"

"Yeah, one of our good customers. He sent you?"

"In a manner of speaking, yes."

He looked through the front window. "You drive a Jeep. What kind of bike do you have?"

"I don't have one at the moment." I said.

"We don't sell motorcycles here, we customize them. So, what are you doing here?"

"I need some background information on Frank Diorio. Did he come here with other people?"

"You see an information sign anywhere here? You need to talk to Frank. Go see him."

"Unless I had a crystal ball and mediumistic talents, it would be very difficult. Frank was murdered a few days ago."

"*Shitte de merde.* I knew I smelled cop. Get lost."

"He was one of your good customers. I need some help to find his killer. I'm not trying to jam you up, buddy," I said.

Leaning forward into my space, he placed his right hand on the counter and with his left gave me the one-finger salute.

"Name's not buddy. It's Tom, and I just told you to get lost."

I stepped to my right, grabbed his outstretched finger, slammed his hand on the counter, and bent his finger upward. With my free hand, I slipped my phone out.

He tried to pull his captive hand back but couldn't. He took a swing with his right hand but found I was too far to reach. When he tried it a second time, I cracked him on the wrist bone with the corner of my phone case.

"Enough of this," I said. "I've been polite so far. You have two choices. We talk here or downtown."

I feigned pressing a speed-dial number on my phone. "Lieutenant Robert Beaudry, I need a squad car for a pickup. I have a hostile witness I need to bring downtown." I added my badge number to the fake call.

"Whoa, whoa," Tom, the Star Wars man said in French Canadian slang, "*Shuck twé pas bonhomme.*"

"I'm not angry. I'm just getting impatient. I expected you to help me solve the murder of a good client."

As if I was still on the line, I told my nonexistent dispatcher to forget the pickup order. All was under control.

A tall skinny guy in green mechanic's coveralls and also sporting a ponytail came to the front counter to ask Tom if there was a problem.

"No, no, everything is fine," Tom said.

Until I saw a cute shorthair brunette come out of a back office, I had wondered if there was an unwritten rule that you had to have a ponytail to work in that store.

"Look Tom, I really don't want to screw up your day. I need your help. We found Frank with his throat slit. His body was in the trunk of an abandoned car. I'm hunting for the punk that did him. You want to help yes, or no?"

"Look, I'm on parole and I didn't report this week. I can't afford trouble. Can you leave me out of this?"

"Not a problem. In fact, tell me what day you should have reported, and I'll cover you saying we had the interview that we're having today."

It was smooth sailing after that. I found out that Frank opted for the 'snake venom' options, had spent a little over six thousand over the sticker price on the new bike that he always came in alone, mostly on a weekend morning, and he was really pissed off about the price he got for his old bike. He wanted something more from the sale. Tom could not contribute more than that.

I left him my card. If you have an issue with your parole officer, have him call me. We parted with a handshake.

* * *

My second stop, the custom paint shop, was in the North West of the city, close to the Pierre Elliott Trudeau airport.

I skipped the tourist routes and took Highway 20 West. It took me a tad less than the GPS prediction of 30 minutes.

The outside signage and window art of the shop were true to its Japanese name.

The hospitality was in stark contrast to the first store.

"Welcome to Miyamoto. What can I help you with?"

I didn't pussyfoot. I did my signature left-hand badge flip move.

"Lieutenant Robert Beaudry Major Crimes Division. I'm here to ask you a few background questions about Frank Diorio. He was one of your customers."

"*Was?* I take it he's dead. I'm so sorry to hear that." He came toward me with an extended hand. I responded with a solid handshake.

"I'm Norman Caron. Everybody calls me Norm. Like in the TV series Cheers. Let's sit in my office."

* * *

We were both installed in visitor's chairs on the front side of his desk. The secretary had served us coffee.

I put my cup on a woven fiber coaster on the corner of his desk.

"Norm Caron doesn't sound very Japanese, yet the store, your ornate lacquered desk and decorations are much in that vintage oriental style."

"I worked in Japan for a couple of years. I fell in love with a woman named Sakura—now my wife. Our head artist here is Asahi Kusunoki. So, there you have it."

I nodded.

"Got it,' I said." Now, back to Frank Diorio. What can you tell me about him? Attitude, background, I'd like to know more about him."

"Can I ask you what happened to him?"

"Not pretty. Slit throat and dumped in the trunk of a car at the airport."

"I'm sorry for him, but to tell the truth, I'm not that surprised his death was a violent one. Frank was a very impolite and aggressive person. He surely made more enemies than friends. If needed, he could show a completely different and charming personality, but it was only a thin mask. I'm afraid that's all I can say about him."

"When was the last time you saw him?"

Norm went to his desk and flipped open a large leather-bound agenda. He rifled through a few pages.

"A few weeks ago. Saturday April twenty-first. He had his bike out from winter storage for only a week or so, and somebody had keyed his gas tank. It was a mess of scratches. He was livid."

"Something an irate woman would do?"

He looked at me sideways.

"I can't give you a professional opinion on that, other than it has 'Prick' and something else I don't remember carved on the other side of the tank. Do you want to see it? I don't think we've started the work yet."

"His Harley is here?"

"Yes, we gave him a loaner," Norm said.

"Ouch."

"Ouch what?"

"I'm afraid you'll not get it back," I said. "He was killed in a field. The bike was set afire, and it's a charred mess. It's evidence from the crime scene."

"We have his fancy bike as a deposit. Can we just keep it?"

Norm stood up and motioned me to follow him. I spoke as we headed into the shop. "In the civil domain, they say that possession is nine tenths of the law. You'd need a legal opinion. I'm just a hunter on the trail of Frank's murderer," I said.

The Harley was a work or art, or more precisely, *was* a work of art. It was now spoiled with tic-tac-toe check marks and meaningless doodles carved deep into the layers of paint. The only legible portion of the scribbles was the word Norm had said in our interview.

"What a shame," was what came to mind.

Norm nodded.

We left the workspace and Norm walked me to the store's exit. He had one hand on the door handle when he said,

"On your question if a woman could have keyed his bike. I just remembered that last year he sold his old bike to a woman and was later seriously unhappy about the deal." Norm said. "Maybe she was too."

I froze in place at his comment.

"He told you this?"

"Yes, maybe a week or so after they came in."

"Whoa, horsey. *They* came in. I think we best sit down again." I headed back to his office. Norm followed me with surprise written all over his kisser.

SEVENTEEN

While replenishing our coffee, Norm's secretary insisted on politically correcting me.

"Executive assistant," she said.

We were back in our same visitor's chairs. This time I had my phone recorder on.

"Tell me again what happened with Frank's old Harley," I said.

"Last spring he told me that was selling his Dyna Super Glide and was looking at a newer, bigger bike and that he would want it fully customized."

I put my palm out as a stop signal.

"Who *he*?"

"Frank Diorio. We had painted his current Harley burgundy and gold flake with a wolf head portrait on the top of the tank."

I rotated my hand clockwise to encourage a speedier and shortened version.

"We took pictures and put his bike up for sale on our website. The next day, a woman called. Said she was interested, but there was no price listed. I told her it was a private sale, that she could meet the current owner here and negotiate the deal. We would inspect the bike for her and give her a written report."

"So what happened next?"

"It thrilled Frank that a woman was the buyer. He changed opinion shortly after the sale. I don't know why, nor do I know the amount or the details of the arrangement."

"You said *they* came in."

I gave Norm the same hand signal to continue the story.

"Frank Diorio came in early that Saturday. We washed and polished the bike. Our head mechanic inspected it and printed out a report. We set the bike up in the showroom. The woman came in around lunchtime. We gave them privacy; they made their deal. She drove it out of our shop. We offered Frank a loaner. He didn't have a delivery date on the new Harley yet and opted to buy the loaner from us with the proviso that we would buy it back. I gave him a special deal, shook on it, and that was it."

"You saw the woman?"

"Yes, a pretty redhead."

I couldn't help blurting out,

"Oh boy."

Norm turned to me, wide-eyed and nonplussed.

"What?"

I turned off my recorder and scrolled to the ghost redhead picture Dobson had sent me.

"Is this her?

"She looks sick, but I'm ninety percent sure it's her." Norm said.

"Not sick. She's not at her best in that picture. She's on a slab in the morgue."

"*Kuso!*—killed too? Murdered?"

I nodded yes.

Norm covered the sides of his face with both hands.

"*Arienai,* not possible. Both the people in the deal murdered."

"That's my challenge," I said. "Do you have paperwork on the sale? Her name and address, perchance?"

Norm reached for his desk phone.

"Suzanne, can you make a print for the Lieutenant? He needs the registration papers on the burgundy Harley that we sold last year for Frank Diorio?"

When Suzanne came back with the file, I nodded to her and said,

"Thank you, Suzanne, thank you, Norm. I appreciate the time you took answering my questions and getting me the sales record. Both of you helped me more than you could know. I appreciate it very much."

I gave my card to each of them.

"You ever get into trouble. Call me before or after nine-one-one. I owe you."

I'm sure they didn't know I was now out of my holding pattern. I was finally going somewhere. I had some solid clues, a name and address for the mysterious Jane Doe, and a link between her and Frank Diorio.

I texted Dobson, giving him the info.

"Our Jane doe is Roxanne Saint John."

I gave him the details from the bike registration.

EIGHTEEN

I drove home with a smile on my face. Pleased with the day and looking forward to a tête-à-tête supper with Pat to celebrate her hard work and her successful legal exams. I called Bistro Luc. Antonio had purchased the restaurant from Chef/restaurateur Luc Fournier. When Luc's aging father began a spiral descent into dementia, he sold the restaurant and moved back to France to be with his parents during their trying time. My friend from the other side of the badge, Antonio Masiello, purchased the business. He kept the original name and the French menu, with the subtle addition of some Italian favorites.

I found Pat sound asleep surrounded by books. Some piled on the sofa, some spread on the floor. She woke when I stepped on that creaky plank next to the reading lamp. Although we did a top-to-bottom renovation, including sanding and refinishing the hardwood floors in a richer tint, the new look and color scheme did not change the house's little quirks inherited during its use since the original nineteen twenty-two construction.

"I'm sorry if I startled you," I said.

"What's the time now?"

"Five thirty-six."

Pat stretched. "I must have dozed off an hour ago. I'm a tad worried. Crackers asked to go out soon after you left, and I've not heard him ask to be let in yet. He's after missing his lunch."

"Probably scored a field mouse or a slow-witted bird. He's surprisingly fast when he wants to."

"We're still on for supper?"

"Absolutely."

"I must look a mess. I'd best put my face on."

"Change nothing. You can't improve perfection."

"You big *muppet, g'wan* with you,"

Pat headed to her bottles, tubes and in whatever jars she supposedly keeps her going-out face. I headed to the patio door to see if Crackers was lurking about. I called him and searched his usual haunts but didn't find hide nor hair of the critter.

* * *

When we entered Antonio's French bistro, Pat led the way, and I trailed behind. Heads tuned to watch us walk to the rear of the restaurant to the owner's reserved table. Patrons perhaps surmised that the big guy was just the bodyguard for some Hollywood royalty. As usual, waiters were falling over themselves in a rush to serve Pat. Maybe her going-out face had an impact, but I suspect her long, flowing red mane and the backless and plunging neckline of her tight black dress also had something to do with it.

Antonio came out of the kitchen, took off his chef's hat, plunked a half-size bottle of Veuve Clicquot champagne on the table, and sat with us.

"I understand you're celebrating good scores on your legal studies," he said. "The bubbly is for you, Pat. I know Robert prefers a red wine."

Antonio raised his right hand, and the headwaiter appeared behind Pat. It startled her when he said,

"What would Madame like as an entrée?"

Pat is not that adventurous with food choices. She stuck to her favorites.

When he asked for my choice, I said,

"Tell the chef to surprise me."

"Speaking of surprises," Antonio said. "I have a new wine I'd like you to try from the Ontario Niagara region. A new offering by winemaker Thomas Bachelder."

Pat said, "I'll go powder my nose before everything is served."

As soon as Pat was out of earshot, I whispered to Antonio, "I got a be-there-or-else invitation to an internal affairs gathering for Monday morning. It seems that our meeting at Diesel's bar has upset someone. We must have been tailed to the club."

Antonio shook his head. "Nobody followed us, trust me. There's another possibility. Give me your key fob. I'll have the Jeep checked."

Pat slid back into her chair, as Antonio headed back to the kitchen.

* * *

Our meals were the usual tasty perfection. The wine was an excellent blend.

To my surprise, Pat succumbed to temptation and ordered a small tumbler of rhubarb trifle.

"It's the season," she said.

Before we left, Antonio texted me on the sly. "Tracker hidden under the rear tailgate spare tire. We put it on one of our supplier's delivery trucks. It'll keep somebody busy and confused tomorrow. Call me when you have time."

NINETEEN

Once home, Pat changed her books from her living room piles to the stack in her corner office.

"I'll be up to ninety again tomorrow. I've still got much cramming for this semester's exam."

"The weather guessers anticipated bright sun and warmth for tomorrow. I'll let you fill your pretty head with legal jargon. If their predictions prove valid, I suggest a brunch break on some terrace on the water's edge."

"That would be brilliant. Now go out and find Crackers. I miss his antics already," Pat said.

I got back empty-handed. Pat was already in bed but wide-eyed.

"I can't find the furry fiend. I went around the block twice."

"I'll not sleep well. I'm used to him cuddling up to me."

"Well, I guess I'll just have to fill in on the cuddling work."

"Work is it now? You big buffoon."

* * *

Sunday morning when I woke, the bedside clock announced four twenty-three, Crackers' usual I want my breakfast time. I don't worry when facing an armed felon, but Crackers' unusual disappearance had my stomach churning. Something was not right in my world.

I slipped from under the comforter and padded to my closet, slipped on jeans and an old comfortable sweater. After walking half a block on my cat hunt, the chill and dampness of the morning gave me a solid clue that I should have added a jacket and perhaps a scarf to my attire. By my third patrol of our neighborhood, the sun cast a fuzzy pink glow across the eastern horizon. Maybe the weatherman was on target. I trudged up the hill from Sherbrooke Street to a street parallel to ours. I was dreading telling Pat that I'd still not found a trace of the missing Maine Coon.

At the bend leading to my street, on a whim, I took the little trail into the park around the Villa Maria School. Twenty feet in, Crackers crawled out from under a hedge. He was missing the tip of one ear, had dried blood covering most of his muzzle and scruff. He walked to me with a visible limp.

If you are on his list of acceptable humans, Crackers will sit on you, or rub against you at any time of day or night, but he doesn't like to be picked up. That morning, there was no push back when I carried him back home.

Pat had tears in her eyes when she saw his bloodied condition.

"Holy saints in heaven. Did he get run over?"

"No, it looks like a fight with another animal."

"He looks in pain. Get him to a vet quick, you have to."

"Sunday, we may have a problem. My usual place is closed till tomorrow," I said.

Crackers tilted and plopped flat on the hardwood floor as if he was out for the count. He did a hacking, chucking-up-a-hairball sound, and a trickle of blood came out of his muzzle. For a moment, I thought it was a death rattle. In my homicide career, I'd had people die in my arms, and I recovered from those events, but today my breathing halted at the sight of him. To see Crackers suffering was knotting my innards. I rushed to get a blanket from our closet, and I wrapped him gently. In the background, I heard Pat at her computer flailing at the keyboard.

She came back to the living room and handed me a sheet of paper from her printer.

"This is the address and route for a twenty-four-hour emergency vet clinic in Lachine. They're waiting for you. Get your arse in gear."

"Yes Sergeant."

* * *

At twenty to six that Sunday morning, it seemed as if I was the only one left on the planet after a horrific plague of some sort. The traffic was nonexistent. I didn't see a single car or human on the trip.

The facilities were modern, and the service was better than in most Quebec hospitals.

The young female vet on duty took one look at Crackers and said,

"*Minou a perdu une sérieuse bataille ?*"

"Yes, I think he had a serious fight with some other animal. I'm not sure who got the worst of it at this point."

My furry fiend was strangely docile with her. His regular vet normally wears heavy gloves and chases Crackers around the room, trying to put him back onto the examination table at least three times per visit.

She petted him under the neck with her left hand as her other examined his paw.

"Your Maine Coon must have done some damage to his aggressor."

"His name is Crackers," I said.

"Crackers, like biscuits, because he likes them?"

"No, like crazy."

"*Ah, bon.* Well, he must have been crazy to *bataille* with a wild animal. He's missing a claw on this side. And he has a broken tooth. He may also have cracked a rib."

I had been worried that he was in such terrible shape that she would recommend putting him down. I was mildly relieved.

She had a cute French accent when she switched to English. To break the tension that had built up in my gut, I commented on it.

"Your accent is from France, not from here," I said.

'France, but what region, if you have a good ear. She challenged.

"Not Paris, not North, nor Marseilles, Perhaps Provence, but my best guess would be somewhere around the center of France.'

"Nantes," she said. "You are very perceptive. Are you a language professor?"

"No, in my job, I interview and study people attentively, including speech patterns and accents."

I did my badge flip move. Strangely, it cast a chill on our conversation. I guess she didn't like cops. I wondered why.

She called in an assistant. She gave him instructions to bring the "patient" to the operating room.

"We will take X-rays to check for internal trauma. I don't think so, but to be sure. Stitches for his ripped claw, some antibiotics and a rabies shot. I'd say he went *Tête-à-tête* with a coyote. We've had a rash of sightings in town this year. We'll keep him for a day to make sure there is no adverse reaction to the meds and anesthetics. Come back Tuesday."

I thanked her and headed out. The receptionist said I'd pay the bill when I'd pick up my cat.

I texted Pat on the way home to tell her the results of the exam, and that Crackers should be back to his usual antics on Tuesday.

* * *

Pat took a break for lunch. As I had promised, we drove to a cute restaurant in St-Anne de Bellevue. We lucked out and enjoyed the sunshine, the splendid view, and the pizza from a patio table on the edge of the water.

Pat was back cramming for her exam two hours and ten minutes later. We both found the house to be quieter than usual.

TWENTY

I woke up later than usual this morning. The cat alarm had not gone off today. Pat had more last-minute cramming for her afternoon exams, and I had a meeting with "Infernal affairs."

The traffic situation heading downtown to headquarters was the usual snarled mess. I've wondered if people are worried their boss had a moment of inspiration during the weekend and realized their job could be done by a less expensive idiot. Everyone seemed in a rush to get to work. Probably to make sure they were still on the payroll, so they could maintain the payments on the five hundred horsepower shiny car they were now driving at nine kilometers per hour down the Decarie expressway.

* * *

I zipped up to the third-floor office. I knew the route by heart. I'd been to Internal Affairs so often the administration was thinking of charging me rent. For years, my nemesis had been Lorn Trehearne, the pencil pushing, rulebook hungry sergeant in charge of the police watchdog department. In the year before his decision to take early retirement, I had got to know him better, without being bosom buddies. We had then tolerated each other with respect.

His ex-partner, the rotund and slow as a snail Simon Whitten, was now in charge. I walked into his office without knocking. He was busy on his computer. Fat little fingers hunting and pecking away at the keyboard.

"Good morning, Simon. I hope I'm not interrupting an important report."

He had put on a few extra pounds since our last kerfuffle.

"You're looking good. Did you lose some weight?"

"Is that one of your smart-assed comments?"

"No, we're not there yet."

I sat in the chair in front of his desk.

"Speaking of not there, why am I here?"

"Let me save this document first, then we'll talk."

"Do you want a coffee? I'll go get some from the machine."

He had a look of consternation and surprise on his face as I stepped out heading to the department's foul brew machine. I guess Trehearne had not warned him about my confuse them with kindness ploy.

* * *

I plunked his cup on the side of his keyboard. There was a seventy percent chance he'd knock it over.

"Careful It's hot," I said.

"There's nothing special," he mumbled.

"The SQ are worried you may interfere with an important investigation into the drug trade. They want assurances you will not overstep your authority."

"I'm looking into a murder. It may have something to do with drugs, but I'm thinking not. They do their job, I do mine. You can reassure them. I'd like to note, however, that both your paycheck and mine carry the SPVM logo."

"Beaudry, for once, I totally agree with you. The top brass volunteered me to act as an arbitrator between the agencies. I'm not pleased about it. You've been unusually nice to me today. Keep it up and inform me first if you feel you've stepped on some toes.

I'll tell you about anything I hear from the SQ side. It seems that they are getting ready for a big raid soon."

"Thanks for the heads up." I took another sip. "The coffee on this floor is better than what our machine dishes out."

I saluted him and made fast for the door.

On the way out of the building, I texted Nico asking if he was free for an early lunch.

He answered seconds later and suggested a restaurant on upper Decarie Boulevard where the old Blue Bonnets race track used to be.

TWENTY-ONE

When I entered the restaurant, it took me a few seconds to recognize Nico.

"Whoa, you're ruining your reputation as a well-dressed man. You look like a college professor at the end of an unruly semester."

"Well, the disguise is doing its job not to attract attention. I'm on a stakeout later today. We have a big drug raid in the west island, a couple streets over from an elementary school."

"We?"

"Joint SPVM and Quebec SQ. We had eyes on that operation before the SQ barged in. They have another raid at the same time on the south shore. They got their lead on this one from that other investigation. Apparently, it's the same gang of wholesalers."

"Are they supplying Diesel's gang?"

'Probably. I'll find out more tonight after we sort out the mess.

"Mess?'

"Typical showboating extravaganza on our side as well as SQ. We'll have the Swat team, three times more cops than we need, and a helicopter. I'm surprised they didn't call for the armored truck."

"Ah, the good old days," I said. "A fast arrest and a slow discussion downtown, no drama. A couple of trusted uniform patrolmen placed at the back door. You and me at the front door with a couple of shotguns."

Our waitress had sidled up to our table while I was talking. She wore the restaurant's uniform, a black blouse, and a short black skirt. The sober outfit contrasted with her very flashy pink lipstick and her ponytailed blonde and green streaked highlighted hair. She stared wide-eyed at me.

"Shotguns at the door?"

I did my badge flip move. Contrary to the vet's reaction yesterday. It produced a wide smile and a thumbs-up sign. We both ordered the daily special.

Between bites, I told Nico I'd call Simon the IA guy and tell him he was right on his comment of this morning.

TWENTY-TWO

After lunch, I headed to the address of last year's Jane Doe murder victim, now identified as Roxanne Saint John. The high-end modern building was in the North-East sector of Montreal Island. The new housing project was above Henri-Bourassa Boulevard and just below Gouin, the last parallel street that follows the river. Some developer must have lucked out on an undeveloped parcel that was probably once connected to the parkland at the water's edge above Gouin.

I slipped the Jeep amongst a line of pickup trucks in front of another five-story multi-condo project under construction. The builder's sign announced prices from four hundred thousand to a million and a half plus for a penthouse unit. Montreal was catching up with Toronto and Vancouver's housing bubble. Where the city will find all the people to fill the myriad of mushrooming condos popping up across town is a mystery. Today, I was concentrating on my own mystery of the two strangely connected murders.

* * *

It took me the better part of an hour and several badge flip moves to find a representative that could help me. I wound up in the two bedroom model apartment for the building under construction with Elisabeth Walbert. She was the head sales person for the project. We stood next to the wallpaper display that showed three-D floor plans for the various condo units. She didn't bother making her sales pitch.

"I'm somewhat shocked and disturbed to meet a detective," she said. "I was told to expect a lawyer from the trustee. I presume that Miss Roxanne is now reported missing."

"Well, your presumption is partly correct in that I need all the information you can give me. We'd better sit somewhere."

* * *

She found us a small boardroom across the street in Roxanne's building.

"I can see the justification for the prices on your project. This is very luxurious," I said. "Let's take it from the top. Where is Miss Saint John's apartment? When did she purchase it, and did she live with someone, would be a pleasant start."

"Miss Roxanne purchased the South facing penthouse nearly three years ago during the building phase. She got a very good price, particularly since she paid in full from her trust account. They automatically pay her condo fees from that same account."

"Trust account?"

"I was not involved in all the details. It was above my pay grade at the time. My understanding is that her family's business in England is in marine shipping. Unfortunately, her parents died in a private plane crash somewhere in Mexico. It was three months after she moved in. Poor Roxanne, she's such a nice girl."

"Did any friends or family meet with her here after the bad news?"

"No, she flew to London for the funeral. I know she has a younger brother. He's handicapped with some debilitating disease. No other family."

"You didn't find it strange she's not lived in her penthouse for close to a year?"

"Not particularly. She had gone on trips to London for several weeks at a time. We never communicated with her. They pay the condo fees on time. There was no need to. The only question we had was this spring, when we did some maintenance, because of some—minor water infiltration in the sub-basement parking where she keeps her vehicles. She must have changed providers. Her phone line was no longer in service. I had to call the trustees in England and ask if we could relocate her vehicles."

"Vehicles?"

"Yes, a convertible sports car, a Jeep, and a motorcycle. That's when they told me they also could no longer contact her and would send a lawyer this week to meet with me."

I opened my badge holder, slipped out a card, and handed it to her.

"If he or she shows up, call me immediately. I also need the information for the trustees in England."

She nodded yes, rummaged in her purse, took out a business card and slid it across the table to me. I fished my phone from my jacket and took a close-up picture. The card had a blue butterfly logo over the legal firm's name. Jones, Adamson, Galkin. Solicitors and higher court Advocates. I'd send them a request for information from my home office later tonight.

"On your last question," she said. "Miss Roxanne has—a—roommate. She's the antithesis to herself. A tough looking older female with tattoos. We haven't seen her in several weeks."

"You've met her? I'd need her name and phone number."

"No, no, I've never met her. I don't know her name. It's just that we had comments from some owners. I saw her on the security cameras."

"I'll need those pictures," I said.

"I'm uncertain we can do that. The privacy of the owners is of utmost importance in our buildings."

"We can cite your firm for hiding evidence in a murder case," I exaggerated.

Her eyes went rounder and her face paled.

"Murder, what murder? I thought you were investigating her disappearance."

"We found Roxanne's body months ago. We didn't know who she was until a few days ago."

She grabbed her purse and held it against her chest as if it was a life vest. Her hands trembled.

"Oh, no, no, such a sweet girl."

"Take a deep breath, hold it for the count of four, then exhale slowly for a count of seven," I said.

Some social worker told me about this stress and anxiety relief exercise years ago. To my knowledge, it's never worked, but I had to say something.

In the following twenty minutes, Elisabeth made six phone calls and DVD copies of the security videos were hand delivered to the boardroom.

The atmosphere in the room was somewhat cooler than when we entered. Elisabeth looked at me as if I had mistreated her. Her saleslady smile had vanished, and her mouth was tight

"I would have appreciated you telling me about her death from the start," she said. "I suppose you want to check out her apartment now."

"Sorry, once the word murder comes into a conversation, most people lose focus. It colors their answers. It makes it much harder to get solid answers. On her apartment, we will provide a search warrant. Make sure that no one enters the premises from today on. No cleaning or maintenance people. The place is now off-limits. Our forensic lab technicians will advise you of how and when they will search her condo. We will not send a team of uniformed police to disturb the owners. Our team will dress in street clothes."

"That's appreciated," she mumbled.

"I'd, however, need to look at her vehicles," I said.

She bent slowly up from her chair as if she was tired from a long travel, or not feeling well.

"Follow me," she said.

* * *

Her Jeep was a 2015 black two-seat Wrangler with only 12415K on the odometer. The sports car was a 350 SLK the model with the Mercedes star on its nose and the roof that slides into the trunk. Its doors were locked. The motorcycle was as described to me. Burgundy, with the wolf head design on the tank, as purchased from the recently deceased Frank Diorio.

I thanked Elisabeth. She gave me a blank look. Feeling that I had outstayed my welcome, I left promptly

.

TWENTY-THREE

As I climbed into my Jeep, my phone rang. It showed the call was from Lorn Trehearne. I had never updated my contact list for my Infernal/Internal Affairs nemesis. I probably would not. Simon, the snail was a mere shadow of his former boss. I didn't think he'd last long in that job. I wondered what this call was about. I answered with my usual opening.

"Beaudry here, talk to me."

"Thanks for the heads-up this morning, Lieutenant. It's a big operation. I've added myself to the raid tonight. I want to make sure we follow all the rules so we don't get nailed with something the defense attorneys can use to unravel the arrests once in court."

"Good for you. Be careful and wear a vest. I'm on another call. I must let you go," I lied.

I hung up and speed dialed. It went directly to Dobson's mailbox.

"Hi Tristan, I'm going to drop off some DVD disks at your office on my way home. I'd need an identification for the woman pictured on the security cameras. She could be a key witness in last year's Jane Doe murder. It appears she was Roxanne's roommate. Get back to me when you can. Tell your husband André that I send my congratulations for winning the set design award for the variety television show."

On the homicide squad, I was the only one that relied on Dobson as part of my team. For most of the others, he was just a lab rat that prepared the technical evidence for the prosecutors. The Montreal police service was still fighting an uphill battle against racism and a homophobic culture within its ranks. That Dobson had a mild stutter and was gay had been a problem to overcome in his professional relations and work environment. I had been an early exception to this and had always kept him in the loop during my investigations. To the dismay of my boss, Tristan and I had become de facto partners. My cases had the department record for most solved and most successfully prosecuted. I was often on television in the news on high-profile cases. Most of the credit should have gone to Dobson for all the "unofficial" work he did for me. I always made sure that I thanked him during my interviews.

For my redhead more than significant other, I could never mention her part in my investigations. When she worked with the fraud squad, she often used her department resources to the benefit of my cases.

Her illicit help stopped last year when she ended her services with the SPVM. We had agreed she needed to concentrate fully on her legal studies. Pat would be articling at the end of this year.

Not sure if she had returned from her exam, I texted her.

"*I hope the exam went well. We don't have any prepared meals. It will be a restaurant delivery supper tonight. What are your desires?*"

To my surprise, her answer popped back near instantly.

"*My desires have nothing to do with food. Order my usual Greek salad with the Gyro chicken.*"

I sent back the thumbs up emoji.

* * *

The table set, and our food was delivered minutes before Pat arrived.

"Great timing. Food's hot from delivery. How was the exam?" I said.

"If I suggest we open a bottle of wine, does that give your man a hint?"

I reached into the fridge and slipped out a chilled Cabernet Sauvignon from the top shelf. I showed it to Pat. She nodded yes.

"Wow, somebody did well today."

"Bloody hard questions and problems, but what I reviewed over the weekend was as if a leprechaun had slipped me the questions beforehand. Brilliant I was today."

I had never seen Pat so hungry. Normally she nibbles and takes her time. Tonight she wolfed down supper and asked what we had for *afters*. Luckily, I had some frozen yogurt that I topped with some caramel sauce and a cherry on top. The dessert disappeared and so did Pat to the bedroom to change out of her now tight skirt.

While she was busy, I got a call from Nico informing me that Simon Whitten was shot during the raid.

TWENTY-FOUR

Sergeant Whitten had asked for me before he entered surgery. Pat was cleaning up the table when I gave her a kiss.

"Don't know when I'll be back. I'm headed to the hospital," I said.

"Whitten, that's the nerd guy, is it?"

"Uh, my bad for calling him that. Yea, he's Treharne's replacement in I.A."

* * *

Nico had told me that Simon was sent to Sacred Heart Hospital on Gouin Boulevard. There was no room at the closer Lakeshore facility.

I zigzagged through corridors, avoiding the rolling stretchers and tired-looking patients parked here and there along the way. I made it to the emergency nurse's station. I got priority response from the badge flip move. The male attendant flicked through his file.

"The other officers are in the waiting room next to B fourteen," he said, as he pointed to his left.

A few more zigzags and I was with Nico.

"I hope I didn't disturb you in the throes of *amore,*" he said.

"Wipe the silly grin off your face. It was a bit early for that. We had just finished supper. What the hell happened?"

Before he started the tale, a patrol officer came in with two cups of coffee. He did a double take when he saw me. He rocked from foot to foot for an instant, gave a cup to Nico, and offered me the other.

"You want a coffee detective?"

I read his name plate.

"Very kind of you to offer your cup, Officer B. Garner. I just finished supper. Keep it."

He sat down, exhaling a sigh. I pointed to the scarred police issue vest next to him.

"Is that Whitten's vest?"

"No, It's mine," Garner answered.

"You may as well tell Lieutenant Beaudry the story. You were there," Nico said.

I sat across from him. Nico stood, sipping his coffee.

"The swat guys had cleared the building. They were all in front, moving out boxes and packages of dope and herding the perps into cars. I was checking out the garden with the I.A. guy. He wanted pictures to show that they were growing pot in the greenhouse."

"It figures," I said. "Sorry, continue."

"Some guy popped out of a basement window, took one look at us and started blasting away with a handgun. I got hit in the vest, dropped to the ground, pulled out my gun, and fired back. The I.A. guy had frozen in place. He took rounds to his vest and a couple in his right arm. He fainted dead away next to me."

"What happened to the shooter?" I said.

"I had hit him at least once. On my radio, I called out shooter. Red shirt heading front. He limped around to the side of the house where a swat guy put him down. He didn't make it to the ambulance."

"Sounds like an action movie. You, okay?"

"An enormous bruise on my left side. SQ was on the scene. They took my weapon, but since they were part of the team. I don't know who will investigate the shooting. My captain said I was clean. That's enough for me."

"Why are you here?" My question got me a longer answer than I expected.

"Had to get checked out, nothing else to do. My girlfriend traded me for some yuppie mid-level boss at her office a couple of months ago. The stupid I.A. guy got hurt on my watch. I need to know if he's okay."

We shook hands after I reached out.

"I don't know what's Simon's condition is. You are more than an okay guy. Pleased to meet you."

Garner had his mouth half open as if he wanted to say something but forgot the words. Nico gave him a thumbs-up sign and a big smile.

* * *

Ninety-four minutes later, an intern strode into our little room.

"If you're waiting for news of officer Whitten, the operations went well. He's out of surgery and we'll send him to a room shortly. I'd suggest you wait till visiting hours tomorrow."

"Operations?" I said.

"Wounds to the upper thigh, hip, and elbow. His body trauma will heal well. The shattered elbow may present a problem. It's too early to tell."

We thanked the doctor.

"Let's go Ben. I'll give you a lift home," Nico said. "Robert, it's not that late. Get back to your redhead that's waiting in bed."

I did, and she was.

TWENTY-FIVE

My plan for Tuesday was first, pick-up Crackers at the vet, then check on Simon in the hospital. I had left a message with Antonio for a lunch discussion to keep him in the loop on my cases and get his updated information on Diesel's gang. Next was a meet with Dobson to set up the search of Roxanne's penthouse and check if he found out anything on the phantom roommate. I also needed to do some shopping and stock up on wine. It would be a busy, but stressless day.

I kissed Pat goodbye.

"I'm off. I should be back for supper," I said.

"I've a bad schedule today, classes from eleven to two in the afternoon. I'll wind up hungry enough to eat a cow between two bread trucks. I'll have a late lunch before coming home. Your man doesn't have to make much of a fuss for supper."

"I'll make you a few munchies just in case," I said as I headed out of the door.

* * *

I was at the vet clinic minutes after opening hour.

The receptionist's elevated desk was at the center of a divided waiting room. The left side was for cats and the right side for dogs. I wondered where someone with a pet reptile would sit.

I walked up to the counter.

"Good morning, I'm here to pick up Crackers, my cat," I said.

The full-figured woman in the frilly pink blouse gave me a big smile and tapped a few strokes on her keyboard.

"Ah yes, the Maine Coon. I can print out your invoice now while you wait. I'm afraid that Doctor Laurent is not in yet. She's normally on time. It won't be long."

She printed out a three-page bill. No wonder she had a big smile.

A young woman with a sad-looking miniature poodle came in. I sat down to check the lengthy invoice. They should have warned me I needed to take a second mortgage on the house. Each line of print was a few hundred dollars per medical or test procedure. While I studied the document, a white-haired elderly man walked in with a mean looking slobbering bulldog. A well-dressed woman holding a short-haired Chihuahua followed him. My side for cats was now outnumbered.

I had inherited Crackers for free during one of my cases. I decided not to argue the four-figure total. I was still ahead of the game for a purebred cat.

The front door flew open, and the French vet lady ran past the reception. The door hadn't yet closed when a police officer ran in, grabbed the vet lady, and shoved her face into the wall that separated the reception area from the offices. He grabbed her by the left arm and the back of her neck and pushed her into one of the examination rooms that ran along the corridor behind the reception desk. When he slammed the door, the sound vibrated throughout the building.

I jumped out of my chair and headed to the door where screams were now coming from.

"Call nine one-one. Tell them you need a supervisor at this address," I said to the startled receptionist.

The exam room door was locked. I heard a male voice yell, "*You bitch, you're not doing this to me,*" followed by more female screams.

I pulled out my weapon and kicked the door at handle level. My weight outclassed the latch. The door burst inward. I stayed partly hidden by the right door frame, badge outstretched in my left hand and my pistol aimed at the uniform cop half turned toward me. He was standing over the veterinarian, who was on her hands and knees on the floor.

"Don't move. If your hand drifts to your weapon, I'll kill you right where you stand. I'm Lieutenant Robert Beaudry from Major Crimes. Get on your knees now, you know the position.

The patrolman had rage in his eyes but complied. Once he had put his hands, fingers interlocked on his head and crossed his legs, I approached. I did the release move and slipped his sidearm from his holster with my left hand. I dropped the magazine from the pistol and racked it open by sliding it hard along my leg. To my surprise, there wasn't a round in the chamber.

I used his handcuffs to bind his hands behind his back.

"You're making a mistake detective, this is a personal matter between my wife and I," he said.

'You just made it public. I holstered my sidearm, pulled out my phone, and took a few pictures of the scene. Veterinarian Laurent was sitting on the floor, tears streaming down her face, one eye swollen half shut and a puffy red welt visible on her left cheek.

"If your wife doesn't file a complaint, I will. For a start, forcible detention, assault causing bodily harm. I'd love you to try adding resisting arrest to the list.'

The cop took one look at my face and lowered his gaze to the floor.

"I've had enough of his shit." Doctor Laurent said, as she wiped her face with the back of her hand.

"When he tried to break into my apartment this morning, I gave him the divorce papers. I have a restraining order, a lot of good that did. He drove up in a squad car with his partner, as if I was a criminal."

I heard someone call out from the reception area.

"Roger, where are you?"

I pulled out my weapon and replied.

"We're back here."

When his partner appeared in the doorway, I had the weapon at my side and my badge out.

"I'm Lieutenant Beaudry," I said as my gun slowly inched up in-line with his crotch. "Take your service weapon out slowly and leave it on the floor. Then go sit on that chair in the corner while we wait for a supervisor."

He looked down. His partner was on his knees and in handcuffs.

"You fucking maniac. Didn't listen to me, did you?"

I did the same, secure the weapon procedure on the partner's gun and put both empty weapons on the exam table. Doctor Laurent was standing unsteadily, leaning on the wall. I pointed to the partner sitting quietly in the corner.

"I think you may have a favorable witness, Doctor."

I pulled my phone from my jacket and thumbed the number for my boss.

"What do you want today, Beaudry?"

"Just a warning call before the shitstorm heads your way."

"*Saint sacramentos*, it's too early for this."

When Jean uses mock French swear words, it doesn't bode well. I plowed on anyhow.

"I'm at," I turned the phone to face the Doctor. She said the name and the address of the clinic. "I've detained a patrol officer for beating up on his wife. There's a restraining, but that didn't stop him from attacking her at her place of work. We're waiting for a supervisor."

From my past blunders, I knew how to preempt IA's involvement and avoid the reams of paperwork they love to burden us with. I told my boss,

"I'll be at headquarters later today for a debrief. This event will be horrid publicity."

Before he hung up, he said,

"I'll advise the brass. This needs a meeting. Call Monique when you come in."

We seem to be in an era where the cops are now the bad guys. Anything untoward we do, pops up on page one and on the suppertime screen. As in any organization, it's a shame that two or three percent of the staff colors the reputation of the other ninety-seven or eight percent of the devoted team.

* * *

When the supervisor arrived with another officer, I gave them the story as I had seen it.

The Doctor, whose name I learned was Charlotte Laurent, chimed in with what had happened this morning and alluded to several other events of abuse that led to the restraining order.

Before the supervisor could comment, I added.

"Your man is in uniform. There are several witnesses outside. I, for one, would like justice done here, but I'm not in favor of negative publicity and newscasts reflecting badly on the SPVM.

This is a marital as well as a legal and a departmental problem. There's a meeting with the brass downtown later today. Just giving you a heads-up, Sergeant."

His eyes became slits, his mouth went stiff and straight. I was certain he knew about the restraining order and of the officer's past family problems.

He gave both his officers the deadly look that a parent gives an unruly three-year-old during a public tantrum.

"You are both on leave for the rest of the day. Further disciplinary action will be taken. I'm removing the handcuffs and driving Roger back to the precinct. We are past due for a one on one talk."

TWENTY-SIX

Crackers was jostling around in his cat carrier, using intermittent howls to tell us how unhappy he was. Doctor Charlotte Laurent was in my passenger seat. We were on the road to my place to drop off my patched up, cranky Main Coon. Then, headed for a lunch meeting with Antonio.

* * *

We were sitting at Antonio's table at the rear of the restaurant. I had told him of this morning's adventure.

"Doctor Charlotte wasn't in any shape to work today. Her husband is still in circulation pending disciplinary measures and charges against him. She's afraid to go home, and I don't blame her," I said. "I told her you could accommodate her in the women's shelter."

"Ex-husband, I filed for divorce last week. He's a violent man." Charlotte said. "The Lieutenant said you oversaw a battered women's shelter."

"The shelter is Robert's creation. I only help administer the facility. My girlfriend runs the daily business. We started it after a bad hostage situation on one of his cases," Antonio said. "Between Robert's and my contacts, we found supporters to fund the purchase of a large old house on the outskirts of Montreal. It's a nice renovated seven bedroom building with a state-of-the-art security system and guards on duty twenty-four seven."

After lunch, Antonio asked for Dr. Charlotte's keys and explained he would later send someone to pick up her car and bring back clothes and personal effects from her apartment. She wrote him a long list. She had to disappear completely until her ex-husband was put away. I saw the killer look he gave her when he left the clinic. In other situations, such a look had been a fair prediction of future violence. Most times, it had been deadly.

TWENTY-SEVEN

My day's plan was now in tatters. I'd drop in to the hospital for a fast visit, then on to headquarters.

* * *

Sergeant Whitten was back in the operating room for an internal bleeding problem, said the head nurse. Visitors are allowed only tomorrow after nine. The news wasn't what I expected, but she told me it was a simple procedure and that he had been doing much better this morning. It automatically ticked off another item on my fractured to-do list.

* * *

At headquarters I headed to the elevators ready to press the button to the crime lab. I wanted to speak to Dobson before wasting my time in a meeting with the brass, but my boss's spooky instant knowledge of when I was in the building dropped that item further down the list. When my phone played its jazz tune, I saw his extension number on the screen. I knew there was no place I could hide. Instead of my usual reply or a simple hello, I answered,

"The meeting is in what room?"

"Small board room fourth floor. Now," he said, then hung up.

* * *

I gave them the breakdown of the officer's attack on his wife as it had unrolled before me. They already had his partner's version, and perhaps from the other witnesses. I knew that Doctor Laurent had explained the whole sad story to her receptionist friend before we left the clinic.

The top brass and our public relations people were gathered to decide if the SPVM would give out the information before it hit the news. Some deaf and blind, desk-bound people doubted it would ever become public knowledge. My boss, chief inspector O'Neil, agreed with me.

"As soon as we lay charges against patrol officer Roger Nestruk, the news hounds sniffing around the courthouse will latch onto the story," he said. "No way this is going be ignored."

Victim Charlotte had had enough of his mistreatment. The storm clouds of her discontent had piled above him. He would now suffer the thunder and lightning of her wrath. I forecasted criminal charges in his future.

As expected, instead of being proactive, the decision was to wait it out. The officer was already suspended would be the reply.

At the end of the meeting, one of the public relations people pulled me aside.

"Where is Doctor Laurent? We can't get her on the phone, and she's disappeared from her home."

"I have her in a safe house. Incommunicado," I said.

"We'd like to speak with her."

I shook my head no.

"Look up the definition of incommunicado."

I left the meeting and headed for the elevator to Dobson's lab.

* * *

When I walked in, I was stunned. Dobson sat in his office behind a cleared desk.

"Your office is immaculate. Where did you hide all your files and papers?"

"Two new four-high lateral filing cabinets a-approved by my boss. New budget year, I think."

"Speaking of new, after all of your filing and clean-up, did you have time to work on the security pictures I sent you?"

"Got to it this morning. Strange results, more g-ghosts on this case. Computer identification system only came up with a seventy-two percent match. The comparative picture that popped up fits the name on the driver's permit used to rent the car where Frank Diorio's body was found in the trunk." Tristan said.

"So that's a good lead. We have a connection, and computers are not always right. I'll take a seventy-two percent clue anytime."

"Here comes the s-strange part," Tristan said. "The woman who rented the car, Miss Monica Tubbs from New York, died in a motorcycle accident in northern Maine three years ago last March."

"Okay, I admit that's strange at first view. But it's just some similar looking impersonator using a dead person's driver's permit," I said.

"M-more bizarre stuff. Your elevator woman has the same arm tattoo as our Jane Doe from last year."

I didn't believe in ghosts, but the tattoos bothered me.

"Maybe the New York lady isn't dead. She just changed her appearance," I said. "Maybe she's the elevator lady and her and Jane Doe were in the same motorcycle club."

"N-no, you can't change the width and position of a person's eyes with any surgery that I know of. Although a good resemblance, the woman from New York and the elevator lady are two different people."

"Okay, unusual I admit, but there's a solid connection between the two women and Diorio on this case. Diorio was such a Lothario he may have scored similar-looking women in both Montreal and New York," I said. "Keep up the good work. I trust you to double-check everything on this. We're not ready to call in the Ghost Buster's yet."

My quip pasted a smile on Dobson's face.

"I printed two of the best elevator woman pictures from the videos. I enhanced and enlarged them so you can show them to others. I sent them to your office, didn't know if you would be in today. I'll send the same ones to your phone."

Before I left the lab, I said,

"I don't know what I would do without you."

That got a bigger smile.

I was in the elevator when my phone beeped. I checked the pictures Dobson sent. Although saleslady Elisabeth had described the roommate as an older woman, the photos invalidated her comment. She was a tall, slim-waisted, athletic-looking woman. Jet black hair cut very short. She appeared perhaps in her late thirties. The full-length photo showed the same tattoos that we had found on Jane doe last year. The flying bird with rainbow wings on her left forearm, and the line of tiny hearts flowing from her ear down her neck to her clavicle.

The people in this case seemed in some way all connected. I had many related pieces. I just couldn't uncover the event that would have glued all of them together.

TWENTY-EIGHT

During supper, Pat gave me a synopsis of her own strange day.

"Crackers is acting oddly. He didn't want to go out at all, at all. He's using the litter box in your bathroom. You'd best clean it up. It's now manky."

Our feline creature slept next to me on a dining room chair. He was curled up into a large ball of fluffy black fur, his white tipped paws hidden under him.

"I guess he's hesitant to go out after having the stuffing knocked out of him," I said.

"He wouldn't let me leave this morning. He wanted me to hold him. He'd howl when I put him down. To sneak out, I had to put a roll of toilet paper in the jacks so he could play at unrolling it."

"That's unusual for him. He normally hates to be picked up," I said.

"Nary the end of unusual for my day. I scored the best on my last exam."

"Not surprised. You've been in the top three nearly all year," I said.

"Not that. The unusual is, I had a phone call at lunchtime from a partner at Stikeman Elliot. They've offered me a position in the firm for my articling, and I'm not even finished my final exams."

"The big litigation firms go after the top students fast, plus your police work must make you an interesting candidate," I said. "Congratulations."

"I'm pleased with the attention, but I don't want to represent the criminals. I want to serve the cause of justice and prosecute the villains."

"It's a very noble thought to want to stop the bad guys from prowling the streets. But this is a great opportunity to learn the other side of the legal system. Some defendants are not necessarily criminal, mistaken identity, poor decisions, coercion from others, they need someone to defend them. It'll give a chance to do some research and earn some bucks while doing it. You can always aim for a prosecutor's job after knowing the ploys used by the opponents. Just saying. It's your choice Pat."

"Not sure I want to spend years of my life on the other side of what I had my heart set on." Pat said.

"In my youth, when I lived with my dad and his brother, we didn't have a television. We had an old radio with but a few stations, and a CB unit to contact the others in the fields or on the tractor. What we had was a wall-to-wall library of books. Through the years, I devoured every one of them. I'll quote one of my favorites," I said.

"On wasting your life?"

"Not wasting but changing. Lailah Gifty Akita, the inspirational author of 'The Alphabet of Success,' said, '*At any time, you realize you are walking on the wrong way, make a U-turn to travel on the right path.*'

"Time, I have. They gave me till next week to think it over."

Halfway through Pat's sentence, my phone started its jazz tune. I let it play while Pat finished.

The screen showed Antonio's number. I slid the green icon and spoke.

"I'm listening. Talk to me."

"There's a hurricane on the way," Antonio said.

"Thanks for the weather forecast. We looking at rain or hail?" I said.

"Neither I'm predicting a serious shitstorm. Call me back on my secure line."

"You look troubled," Pat said. "Bad news?"

"Don't know. I'll be back in a minute. I trotted to my office, rummaged at the rear of my bottom desk drawer, and pulled out the burner phone Antonio had given me last week. I plugged it into my charge station and called him back on the programmed line.

He answered on the first ring.

"I'm on the burner," I said. "What's the panic."

"I sent an old friend to pick up clothes and stuff from the list Charlotte gave me at lunch. He didn't see her ex-husband watching the house. He had most of what she wanted in a suitcase and was going through her dresser when the husband barged in."

"I don't like the sound of this already," I said.

"You'll hate the punch line," Antonio said. "The husband was raging. He figured my guy was Charlotte's new boyfriend and pulled a gun. My friend was an enforcer in the *business*. They struggled, the gun went off, the cop husband is dead."

"Son of a bitch. When did this happen?"

"Twelve minutes ago. I just got the call. My guy will deliver the suitcase to another friend, then he's taking a trip to his fishing lodge way up north on Lake Mistassini until I give him the okay to come back. He has no intention of getting further involved."

"I presume I'll get called on this. If not, I'll stick my nose in because of the incident this morning. I'll keep you informed," I said.

"My guy is a pro. He cleaned and staged the scene as if the husband shot himself in the heart next to her dresser."

"If they put Dobson on it, I'm not certain it will fool him," I said. "We wait it out and see. Just make certain Charlotte is okay."

I got the call five minutes after I hung up with Antonio. I was relieved it was from one of Dobson's assistants. A rotund little guy with no special features, save for a ski-jump nose, and a permanent toothy grin on his face. I had nicknamed him 'the Cheshire man.'

"Lieutenant Beaudry, I really hate to disturb you at this hour, but the Chief Inspector asked me to call you."

"No problem, Officer Shipley, I've finished supper. What is it?"

"We have an apparent suicide in the apartment of Doctor Laurent. I was told you dealt with her and her husband this morning."

"Yes, she didn't kill herself, did she?"

'No, it's her husband, patrolman Roger Nestruk. You should come here before we move the body. I know you like to see the crime scene as it happened.

"I'm leaving now. Text me the address,' I said.

TWENTY-NINE

The details of the staged crime scene impressed me. Antonio's friend must have gained this macabre skill over several years.

In the entrance corridor, there was a decorative row of vacation photographs. All of Charlotte's pictures were scratched out. A larger one of her in beachwear lay on the floor. A fist sized scar in the plasterboard apparent on the wall where the crooked frame originally hung. The ripped half of the picture and shards of glass were spread across the hardwood floor. I noted that some of the larger pieces of frame glass appeared tinged with blood.

I heard voices at the rear of the apartment and headed to the bedroom.

Officer Nestruk's body was lying face down parallel to a low old fashioned six drawer dresser. His head turned facing the room, his right hand, probably holding the gun, was hidden under his body. The left top drawer partially opened, contained woman's lingerie. A copy of the petition for divorce was on the dresser, smeared with tear-shaped drops of blood.

For once, Shipley didn't have his Cheshire Cat grin. He looked serious and worried.

"Our victim died at most three to four hours ago," he said. "Rigor mortis of the face has set in, and his feet are stiff. No rigor of the body yet."

"You look worried," I said. "Why?"

"No suicide note and no exit wound in his back. The bullet didn't go straight through, it went in at an angle and is somewhere in the body. The neighbors reported loud crashing noises, then a single gunshot. I've never seen a person shoot himself purposely that way. It's normally in the head or mouth. Once we see the position of the gun. It will give us a better picture," Shipley said.

One of his technicians rolled the body over. Nestruk held the gun in his right hand with his thumb on the trigger. The front of his thin T-shirt was soaked in blood. We couldn't see the entrance wound, but it appeared as if he had shot himself upwards into the heart.

"He's wearing a "Punisher" T-shirt," I said. "It fits his personality."

"There's no sign of a struggle. It seems as if he shot himself, but something feels off to me," Shipley said.

"He has a bruise and bloodied knuckles on his right hand," I said. "It may be from punching the picture of his wife in the hallway. That would explain the banging noises heard by the neighbors. The only thing that felt *off* this morning was a raging uniformed cop screaming profanities and beating up on his wife. He was off his nut. Had I not been there, you'd be examining *her* dead body."

Shipley shifted his weight from one foot to the other as if he was getting ready for a race or if he was on a heaving and swaying ship in a stormy sea. He still had a worried look on his face. He scraped his bottom lip with his incisors before speaking.

"We'll take our time examining the scene."

"You know your job. Do it by the book," I said. "His death solves a lot of problems for the department. No charges. No dismissal for cause. Just a distressed person who cracked and fell off the edge of sanity. As he clearly demonstrated this morning."

"Convenient for sure, but I have the gut feeling I have to go down to details," Shipley said.

The Cheshire man had been a student of Dobson's. The attention to minor details and the feel of a crime scene he must have acquired by osmosis from years of working with his mentor.

"I agree with you. The situation is unusual. Fingerprint everything in sight. Make sure there was no one else here. If you find nothing, maybe it's as it seems at first glance. Nestruk was an aggressive cop. His record shows several complaints. A violent vain man that didn't want to mess up his face."

Shipley was back to his habit of scraping his bottom lip when worried.

"I have his ex-wife safe in a home for battered women," I said. "You have her apartment for as long as you want. Keep me abreast of your findings. This is in your capable hands. In any case, it solves a lot of department troubles and mountains of adverse publicity."

I headed out of the apartment with a foul taste in my mouth and turmoil in what was left of my tattered conscience, bruised, and battered from years of working in the gutter of human events.

THIRTY

I've been told that I'm politically incorrect. My actions were worse than a simple, improper word. I was once again off the reservation, probably a mile from pure legality, and five miles past the correct police procedures and proper paperwork line. The theoretical line that I had broken through and trampled over too many times during my years of hunting murderers.

I have my own version of justice. I've had it since the age of eight when my mother was gunned down in a botched bank robbery, for which the criminals were never found. For years, I dreamt of finding and facing them down. My sentence would have been dealt out with my dad's old shotgun.

In retrospect, it was obviously the trauma of growing up without a mother, and my angst of having no rhyme or reason for her death, nor any semblance of justice done for her brutal demise, that led me to police work and the homicide squad.

In my first year on the job, I had to gain the trust of some of the lower criminals to reach the dangerous ones. Those who kill without remorse were the ones I would put away. It would never erase my youthful anger, but it would help me find relief and mold my sense of justice and fair play. That's a part of me today.

When I earned a gold detective badge. They paired me with Tall Tony Tondino, a streetwise detective that opted for action, used a liberal interpretation of police procedures and shunned paperwork. I admitted to him that when I was a beat cop; I confronted a known fence and convinced him to give me the stolen goods that a family had reported to me that morning. The deal I kept was, I ignored Marco's involvement as the buyer of the pilfered jewelry. I simply brought the loot back to their rightful owner. No further questions were asked. I filed no report. It got me instant credibility on the street as a straight shooter.

Before cancer took Tony away, we had earned a reputation for solving all our cases. Spurred on by the memory of my mom and of Tony, I've maintained that level of achievement throughout my career. It was a dead-end ride for victim Frank Diorio. On this case, I had only ghosts and no suspects. I worried it may also be a dead end for my reputation of successful prosecutions.

THIRTY- ONE

It shocked me when my boss texted me a lunch invitation for a meeting out of the office. In all the years under his command, this was a first.

A sleepy-eyed Pat joined me in the kitchen.

"You babbled unintelligible words as you tossed and turned most of the night," I said.

"I didn't sleep much. The hounds were chasing a fox in my dreams. I think I was the fox. I'm mulling the decision to take the internship or not. Did I keep you awake?"

"No, I had my own toss and turn dilemma on the case I'm working. I should have dreamt of a big bad wolf, not a mere fox," I said.

"My man's in a serious muddle, I'd guess."

"I may have done a few low deeds. Maybe I need some legal advice, perhaps from a soon-to-be lawyer. One with red pillow hair and sleepy eyes."

"Pillow hair?"

"Cute disheveled pillow hair. I'm between the floor and the carpet, and I fear a potential posse of people will shortly walk through the room over me."

"Your after telling me, under the carpet, that low are you now. You'd best come clean," Pat said.

"I told you about my run-in with Officer Nestruk when I picked up Crackers. He was beating up on his wife. He's now on leave pending an investigation, so still on the streets. I was worried he may go after her before she can officially bring charges. I met with Antonio, and we placed her in our abused women's shelter."

"Protect the victim from further harm, *shure'n* the priority. *Fair play to you*," Pat said.

"Here's where it gets sticky. She gave us a list of clothes and sundries she needed from home. Antonio sent an old friend to get her stuff. While he was in the apartment, Nestruk showed up in the same crazy mood of that morning. He went ballistic and pulled a gun, accusing the guy of running away with his wife."

"Your man's a *whopping git*," Pat said. "*Mayhaps*, not playing with a full deck."

"That's his problem. My moral and legal dilemma is that during a fight for the weapon, it went off, killing officer Nestruk. Antonio's friend from his criminal days staged the event as a suicide and has pulled a David Copperfield vanish trick. The Cheshire man called me to the scene and has reservations about the apparent suicide. I stayed mum on what I know. I told him to fingerprint everything in sight and if he can't prove somebody else was there, let things be as they appear. I don't want to implicate Antonio or his friend, yet I don't feel right about withholding evidence."

"One of my professors gave us an analytical trick. To set priorities in a list of potential evidence, take one piece away from the pile to see what happens," Pat said.

I handed her a gluten-free blueberry pancake and filled her coffee cup.

"You lost me."

"How did you find out about the fight and the shooting?"

"Antonio told me," I said.

"So, not prima facia evidence. It's second-hand hearsay. If I was a defense lawyer, I'd exclude your testimony. Subtract yourself from the equation. You never had that conversation. What would happen?"

"The technical team and Shipley, probably without his usual grin, would do what they do best," I said.

"Primus, you are worrying about an event that may never happen. Secundus, your testimony is as useful as a cigarette lighter on a speeding motorbike. Tertio, do we still have some of the low-cal maple syrup?"

"No wonder the big firms are after you. You think like a lawyer, you speak legalese, you're there. You're correct on your evaluation. How much do I owe you for the consultation?"

"Well, my back is stiff from all of my tossing and turning."

The after-breakfast back rub went into overtime with a bonus front rub. We both had to rush to shower and dress to meet our daily schedules.

THIRTY- TWO

I met my boss at the fancy French eatery above the Contemporary Art Museum of Montreal. A short walk, two-blocks West from our headquarters.

I climbed the wide circular staircase to the restaurant area on the second floor. The maître d' led me to a table placed along the half circle of window wall. O'Neil had his right hand around the stem of a balloon wine glass. The fact that I was sixteen minutes late was apparent from the burgundy dregs left at the bottom of his drink.

"Upscale place. Is this on your expense account?" I said.

Jean's mustache was near straight. A fuzzy gray caterpillar at rest. I couldn't tell if he was in a serious mood, or it was his usual snarky attitude for something I did wrong or didn't do right according to the rules.

"Why are we meeting out of your office?"

"Too many curious ears. We're here to discuss an-off-the-record favor I did for you. Lunch is on me. Regulations state that a subaltern officer cannot pay for a superior's lunch. It would smell of bribery."

"This meeting is already beginning to smell of last week's un-refrigerated halibut." I said.

"That's exactly what the two provincial police detectives said about you."

"Whoa, horsey. Where did this come from?"

Jean summoned a waiter by simply raising his forefinger. We accepted his recommendation of the special of the day and more wine.

My boss continued his story once our glasses were refilled, and the waiter was out of earshot.

"The SQ, in full pompous ceremony, raided Diesel's hangouts, his residence, and found nothing. No illegal weapons or substances. The drug dog didn't even catch a sniff of anything in the three places they hit."

"Diesel's wife Sophia likes a clean place," I said.

"They had a different opinion. Their premise is that you warned the gang during your several meetings with their leader."

"I was never in the confidence of the SQ. I couldn't have known about the timing of the raids. It's bullshit."

"Logic does not seem to frame any of their suppositions. They decided that you're a crooked cop. They investigated your finances and real estate dealings and found unexpected riches. Payoff from the motorcycle gang is suspected."

I said, "What?" a little too loudly. It startled the middle-aged, rotund lady at the table behind me.

Jean apologized on my behalf. He held his hand palm forward and mouthed "*pardon*" to her.

"I told them about the insurance inheritance from the unfortunate death of your ex-wife Colleen, and of the women's shelter you generously used most of it for. Since they had no warrant or legal basis for their search, nor had they keep us in the loop, I threatened to raise an interdepartmental stink that would put a squad of dozen skunks to shame. I made it clear, if they pursue their harassment of one of my officers, it will not be in their best interest."

"I'm glad you didn't invite me to that meeting. There would have been a lot of blood to wipe up," I said.

"I know you forget the *official* rule book. Here and there," Jean said.

"Mostly there," I said.

"Don't interrupt me. I told them to get out of my office and not darken my doorway again."

"A bit cliché, but I presume it worked," I said. "I really appreciate you going to bat for me."

"It's not the first time, Lieutenant. Don't push your luck."

When my boss uses my title and not my name, it's time to stop talking shop. I took a sip of wine and did the logical thing. I changed the subject.

I told Jean about Pat's dilemma of an offered job on the defense side of the legal system. His comment was. "If you were a CIA operative, and the KGB offered you a no strings attached visit to their spy school, would you refuse? Learn everything you can in life. You never know what you may need farther down the line."

"That's what I told her, in different words," I said.

"While we're speaking of good family news, my artistic niece on Irene's side is having a showing on Sherbrooke Street, near Guy Street. It's opening this Saturday at ten a.m. Be there."

He reached into the inside pocket of his jacket and handed me the advertising flyer and two tickets for the event.

"Yes, sir. It will give Pat a break from her studies," I said. We finished our meal, and we both skipped dessert.

THIRTY- THREE

My Jeep slept peacefully in the reserved parking at headquarters. I returned to the lot alone. Jean took the rest of the day off to drive Irene to the Cedar's oncology center. His wife had a follow-up blood test and exam. She was now in remission from her breast cancer after a hard stint of double dose chemo eighteen months ago.

I let my Jeep snore for an hour more. I rode the elevator up to Dobson's lab. He was typing a report on his computer.

I shook my head at the sight of him. Fingers thrashing at the keyboard, and a slice of what looked like a ham and tomato sandwich dangling from his partially closed mouth. The other uneaten half, leaking mayo on his mouse pad.

"Tristan, you should know, having a rushed meal while you work is not good for the health."

"I'm b-buried in reports to be done."

"Take a three-minute break. Nobody will keel over in pain if they get a file a few minutes late. Do you want me to get you a fresh coffee?"

"Diet cola."

A few minutes later, I handed him his soft drink. His report, and the ham and tomato sandwich, were both finished. Tristan pushed his chair back. He looked pale and haggard. I removed a stack of crime scene pictures from a visitor chair and sat across from him.

"You look tired, buddy. You, okay?"

"André's contract with the television show has ended. The–the series is not being renewed."

"Your husband is an award-winning artist. He'll find something else. Don't worry yourself sick. We need you,"

Dobson's face was still pale and drawn, but his eyes lit up.

"I did more research on t-the elevator lady," he said. "I ran the pictures through all our databases. Didn't find ah anything to identify her. She doesn't have a driver's license or a Medicare card, or a Canadian passport. N-nothing with an official picture on it. Nothing, zero. Very strange."

"Diorio's body was in the trunk of a car rented by a deceased New York resident. Somebody is using her I.D. Ten to one, our mystery lady is not a Canadian. We have a U.S. connection in this case," I said.

"I, I befriended an American coroner I met at a seminar years ago. We're still on a technical Face Book group together."

"Reach out Tristan. You never know when the next clue will pop up."

I thanked him for the work and research before I left his lab.

* * *

I headed home intending to prepare some tapas type bite sized appetizers for a midnight snack with Pat. She had evening classes today.

Normally, she was still in full attention mode when she came home. Pat needed some time to unwind before she could sleep. Halfway to the grocery store, a call replaced the blues song playing from the Jeep's speaker system.

"It's Tonto. Call me when you have a minute." Antonio's gruff voice instructed.

His allusion to Tonto, code for off-the-reservation business. Call me back meant on a secure line.

I skipped the shopping. Something was awry, and I needed to find out what.

THIRTY-FOUR

Sitting in my office, I dialed Antonio's unlisted number from the burner phone.

Not a man for idle chit-chat. He didn't bother with. Hello, how are you?

"Someone is gunning for you," he said.

"What else is new?"

"Take this seriously. Diesel thinks one of his men got drunk and talked about the—incident that night in the front of the bar. He was one of the guys picking up the shotguns. He told the wrong people that you offed a rival gang member."

"They sent someone to kill me. He's the one who's dead. The same happened to the assassin before him, and the one before that," I said.

"Don't think you're bulletproof. Your luck may run out some day. If you see a shadow behind you for the next few days, it'll be me as backup," Antonio said.

"They probably know you were involved. You'd best be careful as well. Your name is written just under mine on the kill contract."

"I know. But I don't have to abide by the rules. You do. I've called a few old friends of mine. Diesel will get back to me with some names. I'm planning to go proactive on this. You do your police thing. I'll do my thing."

Unceremoniously, Antonio hung up.

Well, never a dull moment. The 1979 credit card ad for American Express don't leave home without it would now apply to me. Not for a card, but for body armor.

I had used the burner phone several times. As per Antonio's recommendation when he gave it to me. I pulled the SIM card and snapped it in two. He would provide a new one the next time we met.

When I hid the burner in my desk, my "official" phone buzzed from next to my laptop. It showed Nico's number.

"To what do I owe the honor of this call?"

"Carmen and the girls are out this evening for her cousin's baby shower," Nico said. "Also, I heard rumors on the street about a bounty on your head. I figured you may need back-up."

"Very kind of you. My back-up is under my left armpit as usual. The rumor is true. Pick me up at home. I'll tell you the story at supper. You'd better wear a vest," I said.

"I hate to wear the Safe Vest in summer. It spoils my slim look."

"There may be collateral damage around me. Bullets have no conscience or morals," I said.

"*É vero*. A vest it is. I'll be at your door at six."

* * *

Nico drove us to a little Italian restaurant in the north-east end of Montreal, just off from Lacordaire Boulevard. I went with the *tartaro di manzo*. They served the tartar of filet mignon with crouton strips, a salsa dip, and an interesting tangy red sauce that when I inquired, the waiter told me it was a secret recipe from the chef's grandmother.

Nico opted for the *farfalle con tonno*. The pasta was home-made and the tuna fresh from the day's market shopping. We enjoyed our meal and a bottle of Trevini Primo Merlot. We chatted about the job and our family. I told Nico of the gun play in the parking in front of Diesel's club.

"They sent a team and only one comes back. I guess the *chooch* didn't get the message," Antonio said.

"Our mutual friend Antonio has elected himself as my bodyguard and warned me he'll go proactive on this."

Nico did a hand gesture that I was not familiar with.

"*Probabilmente*, we'll see his results on the six-o'clock news."

"It's the first time since I've known him to be on the war path. Whoever ordered the hit may just vanish," I said.

Nico insisted on picking up the bill.

We walked a half block to the east toward Nico's maroon Charger. The first shots rang out before we got to the car.

THIRTY- FIVE

Criminals rarely bother with target practice. Lucky for us. Shooting at zig-zag running and diving targets from a moving vehicle gave them another disadvantage. By the second shot from the red pickup truck, we were prone on the sidewalk, hidden behind some unfortunate person's Nissan Pathfinder. Both of us had the same street-smart dive to the ground reaction as soon as we saw the slow-moving decked-out club cab. Big tires, purple lights from under the running boards, windows open, but no rap music playing. The something-was-wrong feeling was amplified as soon as the barrel of a pistol stuck out from the passenger side window.

Over us, the dull sound of bullets punching holes in the car was mixed with the tinkle of the hailing glass fragments from the Nissan's windows. None of their errant shots were hitting close to us.

They were ill-equipped for a drive-by shooting. They had no automatic weapons.

We took advantage of a sudden lull in the firing to jump up and show our displeasure.

Nico ran a few feet ahead and crouched in cover behind the base of a metal street light post. He promptly put four or five rounds into the front windshield of the truck. On my side, I was on my knees firing through the Nissan's now empty front side window frames. My hand steadied by resting on the door frame, I aimed at the nose of the rear shooter and pulled the trigger twice. The truck slow motion drifted to the curb and hit Nico's light post hiding spot as he dove to the right. The fireworks were over in less than a minute.

We cautiously approached the Ram pickup truck. I covered Nico as he peeked into the driver's side. He slid his left palm across his throat.

"They're all out of action," he said.

I called 911 to report the officer-involved shooting. Nico called his boss Lieutenant Falco from the anti-gang squad.

THIRTY-SIX

Lieutenant Falco's hard-set jaw and fists on his hips indicated that he wasn't happy.

"Every time you two get together, it's a sloppy remake of 'Bad Boys II'. This is the worst of your scrapes yet."

"We were just having a friendly supper together," I said. Before I could add another comment, one of the patrol officers brought a clear plastic evidence bag to Falco. After glancing at it, he held it up in front of my nose, flipping it front and back. It held a wrinkled sheet of paper with my picture on it. On the reverse side, written in ink, was the notation $25,000.

"Beaudry, I should have known you were the prime target here."

"Prime may be the wrong adjective. A measly twenty-five grand. It's insulting," I said.

* * *

As required, we had turned over our sidearms to the tech squad. There would not be an official comment from the police tonight. So far, it was being treated as a gang-related shooting. To keep us away from the paparazzi, Falco had instructed us to go get a coffee and to stick around until further instruction. I had left a message on Pat's phone with an understated explanation about a recent shooting incident.

I was on my second cappuccino and my fourth biscotti.

"I should have switched to decaf."

"Cappuccino is a morning-only drink in Italy. Don't make it worse," Antonio said.

The caffeine was balancing my adrenaline down from after the gunfight.

Falco had placed an officer at the door of the restaurant, denying entrance to the newshounds or anyone else. It surprised me when it swung open.

The wispy haired blonde apprentice technician from the crime scene in the swamp came bouncing in with a smile, a swishing ponytail, and a large format Apple tablet. She wore light gray leggings and a cut-off pink t-shirt showing four inches of midriff. Not the usual look for a police technical lab employee.

"Good evening, Lieutenant." She fixed her eyes on Nico while she spoke to me.

His handsome Italian playboy look has that effect on many young inexperienced women.

"I'd introduce you," I said. "But I never got your name."

"Sondra. The lab called me while I was jogging."

Nico half rose from his seat and extended his hand.

"Sergeant Nicolas DiLalla antigang Squad."

She turned to me as she swiped the screen awake and placed the iPad in front of me.

"We took this from the driver's phone," she said. "Lieutenant Falco wants to find out if you know this man."

It was an out-of-focus picture of Antonio. He was partly in shadow and wore his pulled-up baklava mask on his head. Probably taken on the sly during the gunplay in front of Diesel's bar.

I pursed my lips and shook my head no.

Sondra swiped the screen again. Another fuzzy picture slid onto the screen. This time it was of me leaning against my Jeep.

"Can't say anything about the first picture, but I'm pretty sure I recognize this handsome—devil. I saw him this morning while shaving."

"You appropriately put the accent on, devil," Nico said.

Sondra snickered. "This may interest you." Her third swipe put a copy of an e-mail on the screen.

The gist of the text was a one-hundred-thousand-dollar bounty to anyone that would kill either of the men featured in the attached pictures.

"Thank you," I said. "I feel much better now."

Sondra looked at me with a puzzled look.

She said. "Lieutenant Falco said you can go home."

We did.

THIRTY- SEVEN

During our drive back, we reviewed the night's events.

"I don't understand why our antigang team didn't get intel on this attempt before the shootout," Nico said. "I wonder who set you up."

"I'll give you a hint. Maybe my friendly motorcycle gang leader Diesel isn't friendly at all."

Nico lowered his head. He looked at me as if peering over reading glasses.

"Diesel, set you up?"

"Sondra showed me pictures of Antonio and I from in front of Diesel's club. A close-up pic right after the attack and gun play. It had to be one of his men who snapped it."

Nico put his palm down and feigned biting the side of his index finger as if his hand was a sandwich.

I wasn't familiar with that Italian gesture. I was, however, quite certain it wasn't complimentary.

"I can't help you much with this," Nico said. "I'm already on Falco's watch list for a search and seizure I did without the proper paperwork."

"You did enough tonight. I wouldn't have been able to fight all three of them. Just don't tell Pat the gory details," I said. "I'd best call the other guy on the kill list. They emailed a dozen trigger-happy punks looking to score the one hundred K."

I picked up my phone and speed-dialed Antonio's gym number.

"I want to make a reservation for tomorrow morning at opening time. The message I left on his answering machine was a code for "I need some time with the heavy punching bag".

THIRTY- EIGHT

Once home, I sneaked into the sliver of space left between a face down spread-eagle Pat, and my cross-bed stretched out disheveled Crackers.

As usual, the furry purr-machine woke me early by rubbing his head against my chin. It was his breakfast time. I fed him and prepared people food.

This morning's breakfast was a disaster. It ended with Pat in a foul mood and tears in her eyes.

As I was telling her about the minor and insignificant events of last night, Crackers accidentally clawed a deep scratch on Pat's thigh while trying to steal a piece of crisp bacon from her hand.

"You're acting as if nothing happened. You downplay everything bad. You're not protecting me at all, at all. I'm so scared they'll call me some day to identify your body, and I'll never ever forgive you. You're thick as a brick sometimes, you big dope. I'm off to patch myself up. I'm bleeding all over."

Occasionally, I realize how stupidly childish I am about women, and many other things in life. As an excuse, I could say that I was raised by my dad and his overly macho soldier brother. I didn't have a mother, nor any other female influence, until I went to the police academy. The truth is that I'm stupid. I need to work on gaining a wider point of view from my limited bull in the china shop street attitude and cultivate more empathy.

It ripped a tear in my heart when I heard Pat sobbing in the bathroom. I barged in, picked her up, and held her tight in my arms. She tried to wiggle away in the first second, but then seemed to melt into me.

"I'm going to get a swat team officer as a bodyguard, and I'll take a long weekend until this blows away. We know who's responsible, and he'll be off the streets in a few days."

Her tears had dried, and she had a hint of a smile when she finally pushed me away.

"Off with you now. I have to get dressed. I have a meeting with the personnel manager for Stikeman Elliott. I want to find out more about the proposed job before I decide if I accept their offer."

I kissed her on the nose.

"Good luck. I'll back you up on whatever you choose."

While she got ready, I went to my office, took my messages, and checked my email. Most of it was ads for furniture, lamps, or small kitchen appliances that Pat had searched for and purchased months ago. One message was from some guy in Dubai. I hovered over it, ready to drop into the spam folder. I hesitated when I noticed the blue tinted butterfly logo. I remembered the business card I had photographed while I was with Elisabeth Walbert, the sales lady from Roxanne's building.

I opened the message. It was from a Mr. Gateley of Jones, Adamson, Galkin, the British trustee firm. The summary of his reply was apologies for a late reply, and deep shock to hear of his client's murder. He would be in Montreal for the next three days at the downtown Westin Hotel. He left me a cell number.

Seven ten A.M. was early for a business call, but I dialed his number anyhow. I'd leave a message.

To my surprise, he answered on the first ring.

"Francis Gateley, good morning."

"Lieutenant Beaudry from the Montreal police. I hope I didn't wake you."

"Not at all. I was just leaving for the day. I remember you're the officer that sent me the bad news about Miss Roxanne. We must meet."

"The exact reason for my call," I said. "When, where?"

"I'd be free at tea time this afternoon. The reception desk at the hotel restaurant will know where I am seated."

"Thank you," I said. "See you then."

He said, "Cheers." And hung up.

I was hoping the representative of the law firm would give me more insights into Roxanne's life and travels. You never know when a clue will pop up and solve the case.

THIRTY-NINE

I was showered, dressed, and wearing my silent partner protective undershirt. I was ready for a new day and come what may. Pat was all dolled up for her meeting. She didn't allow me to hug her. It would muss up her outfit. I bowed and kissed her hand.

"Go forth and slay the dragon of injustice, my lady," I said.

"You big *omadhaun*. Get yourself to work now."

"Going to the gym first. Then a meeting with your uncle."

* * *

I'm uncertain if the saying, "Early to bed and early to rise makes a man healthy, wealthy and wise," is still valid in this time and world. What is true in Montreal is if you're ahead of the morning traffic hour, you'll zip around the orange cone army and get wherever you're going on time and with fewer hassles.

Antonio met me in the reception area. I showed him the pictures of him and me taken in front of Diesel's club.

"This is old news. A friend sent me that picture and an email putting a price on our heads this morning," Antonio said. "I never really trusted Diesel. More so since he seems to have disappeared into the woodwork."

"If it's him that betrayed us, he's a very adroit conman. He and his wife talked to me at length. I'm extremely surprised he put a price on us," I said.

"I have three old buddies that came in from New York. Antonio pointed to his office door and said, 'I gave them the job of finding our supposed friend. In the meantime, tell me about the shootout on Jean Talon Street."

I did. In his former hit-man profession, he'd been in that situation before with worse odds. It did not impress him.

"Good thing your friend Nico was there. Now he's in the game with two points for saving you."

"It's not a game," I said.

"Life is a game Beaudry. It must be played with skill and with gusto."

On that strange philosophic comment, I left for my boss's office.

* * *

To my surprise, Chief inspector Jean O'Neil's office was empty. I walked to his secretary's cubicle twenty feet away.

I've been reminded a few times that the politically correct title is now executive assistant. After implementing the new organization chart, Monique had told me, "The only changes with the new fancier terminology is more work, and more computer skills required for the same pay grade."

I popped my head into the dragon's lair.

"Good morning, *Madame* Monique."

She didn't stop or even slow her typing pace on the keyboard.

"Go away. I'm busy."

"I have a sit-down with the boss. He's not in his office."

"Called to a special meeting upstairs. Won't be back till after lunch and maybe later. Next time, call ahead."

"All that fast typing must make you thirsty. You want me to get you a fresh coffee?"

"What do you want, Beaudry?"

"Just tell him I was on time."

"Black but bring two packets of sugar."

* * *

The spring-cleaning bug must have bitten me. I used my new-found free time to finish some past due paperwork, put my files in order and clean up my desk. I checked in with Dobson. He had nothing new on our mystery lady from the security camera pictures at Roxanne's building.

* * *

I'd be early for tea time, but downtown rush hour had started an hour ago. I fact, Montreal no longer had a rush hour. Main streets and boulevards were bumper to plastic bumper from after lunch to seven-thirty in the evening.

The Weston hotel had taken over the old Gazette building. It was now one of the city's high-end facilities. I left the Jeep with the parking attendant, who lost any chance at a decent tip when he burnt rubber, zipping it down to the basement lot.

The hotel restaurant/bar is aptly named the Gazette in memory of the building's newspaper history.

The slim oriental woman at the reception desk had a big, welcoming smile. She picked up a menu from the stack behind her counter as I walked in.

"I'm early for a meeting with one of your guests. A Mr. Gateley," I said.

"Not too early. He's already seated. Follow me."

I did.

Gateley's appearance wasn't what I expected. He didn't look like the traditional English proper and mousy lawyer that I had imagined. A wiry man with big hands, a head full of wavy gray hair and a broken nose. He looked like a street fighter in a Harrods business suit. He was scribbling notes in a cream-colored leather-bound note book. A pile of legal sized document spread around him, held in place by a near empty martini glass.

"Good afternoon, Mr. Gateley."

He nodded, stood, shook my hand, picked up his stack of documents, aligned them and glided them gracefully into a slim briefcase of the same tint and leather as his notebook.

We both sat down. "Nice case," I said.

"A present from a client in Dubai. Speaking of clients, I was very distressed at hearing of Miss Roxanne's violent and premature demise. Can you tell me more?"

"You sure you want to know the gory details?"

"I'm not squeamish. I'm the firm's trouble shooter. I'm certain I've seen and heard worse. It's tea time. Do you want a libation before we begin?"

"What happened to tea and mini sandwiches?"

"Changed to wine and bar snacks years ago," he said.

He grabbed the menu and wine list that the reception lady had placed on my side of the table, scanned it briefly slid it back to me, he suggested an aged Brunello Di Montalcino.

"Can't go wrong with a hundred- and sixty-five-dollar bottle of Italian artistry. I think we'll get along fine," I said.

FORTY

I gave lawyer Gateley the story of how we found a Jane Doe body and of finally discovering she was Roxanne St. John. He wrote it down in his fancy notebook.

"Why do you need all these ugly details?"

Gateley took another not too delicate gulp of his wine.

"For several million reasons," Gateley said. "The family insurance policy has added benefits depending on the nature of her death. Also, her father was a *very* wealthy man. As a deterrent, there's even a clause that provides a million-dollar reward for the capture and prosecution of any criminal who kidnaps or hurts any of his family."

"The shipping business must be very lucrative," I said.

"The Saint James group is more than shipping," Gateley said. "They specialize in logistics, ships, fleets of lorries, refrigerated storage facilities. They even have an arrangement with commercial airlines for blocks of weight and flight time across the globe."

Although we didn't order, the waiter brought a plate of sliced vegetables and three types of dips, as well as slices of artisan bread.

Gateley continued,

"Fatefully, her parents died before she did. They would have been shattered at the news of Roxanne's senseless murder.

I raised my glass.

"Here's to justice being served. Unfortunately, I won't be eligible for any reward, it's part of the job I'm paid for. My capture and prosecution rate is one hundred percent, and I'm close to finding Roxanne's killer."

"How close?" Gateley said.

"I'm working on the murder of a criminal biker that's somehow tied in with Roxanne's. I pulled out my phone and swiped to my picture file.

I'm looking for the woman who was living with Roxanne." I bent the phone towards him.

He gave me a crooked, false smile as if I was a disobedient child or an adult idiot.

"That's Roxanne's wife."

"Wife?"

'Yes, we found out when Roxanne came back to Bolton for the funeral. I had known for years, but she only came out after her parents passed. Her straitlaced mother would have had a heart attack and probably would have pushed for disinheritance.

"Well, the wife has vanished. She's no longer in the penthouse. We find no records nor trace of her in Canada. I don't even have her name. What can you tell me?'

"She calls herself Claudette Fay. Her real name is Claudia DiFeo. She has an Argentinian passport. She lived with another woman in New York who died some four years ago. I can get more background for you from my office. Roxanne changed her will after the marriage. Claudia stands to inherit eight million dollars. You tell me she's disappeared. I hope she's not in danger," Gateley said. "That would be another sad tragedy."

"The connection to New York I have. Miss Monica Tubbs from New York crashed and died in a motorcycle accident in Northern Maine three years ago last March. Someone else is using her identification."

"I'm not the detective," Gateley said. "But I'd hazard a guess that Claudia is using her ex-girlfriend's papers."

"This is feeling like a conspiracy and a motive for murder. Does Claudia A.K.A Claudette know about the eight-million-dollar inheritance?" I said.

"No, she does not. The will was sealed. We had strict instructions to open it only in the event of her death, which we did after you informed us. In light of his wealth, Roxanne's father was very cautious about con men, profiteers, and scammers. He taught his daughter well. I'd wager that Claudia knows nothing of this windfall."

I drained the last drops of the fine wine after munching on a dipped snow pea.

"Well, there goes that theory."

We finished with small talk and a promise to keep in touch.

FORTY- ONE

Before I left the hotel, I texted Pat to inquire about her interview. She answered by phoning me.

"Brilliant it was. I accepted their offer, and they kicked in a signing bonus. I've a late class, details at home later."

"You sound pleased. It makes my day. I'll put a bottle of bubbly in the fridge for a late snack."

"*That's the dog's bollocks.* Later, love." I heard traffic in the background before she hung up.

When Pat was displeased, unsure, or happy, she'd slip into her Dublin slang. I understood sixty percent of it, the rest I guessed, mostly in the conversation's context.

I still had the phone in hand when the screen showed Antonio's number.

"Time for a fast-evening workout back at the ranch," he said, then hung up.

I took it as, be at the gym *fast*. The fast was impossible at this time of day, but I would be there. I was stuck in the midst of the ambling herd of metal steeds headed back home from downtown offices.

Fifty minutes later, I was face to face with Antonio on the other side of the building's glass entrance door. He unlocked it, didn't say a word, but gave me the behind the back military hand signal to move up.

His gym is on the top floor of a small pizza shop. We were in a corridor that ran next to the restaurant. We headed to what looked like an emergency exit with the traditional panic bar. He pushed it open to reveal a wide landing with a fire door leading to outside on our right, and another metal door on the left with a keypad lock. He pressed a few numbers, and the door opened to stairs leading down.

"Didn't know the building had a basement," I said.

"When I sold my first gym next to the shopping center to a franchise. I purchased this building during construction and added a few personal touches," Antonio said.

The sub-floor corridor led to several closed metal doors. We entered the first on our left.

The room was bare concrete, the grain and outline edges of the wood forms reverse printed in the cement. Three metal chairs at the far end of the space had their legs imbedded into the concrete floor. The same principle applied to the table in the center and to the two facing chairs across it. The place was lit by explosion-proof wire mesh lighting along the walls. There was a video camera on a tripod in the far corner. The decorator must have been a dungeon master.

I recognized one of Diesel's men chained by the wrists to the metal ring protruding from the center of the table. He looked ill and unhappy, as if recuperating from a drunk.

Two other men were in the room, both in expensive-looking business suits. Antonio did not introduce them. A man with a Santa Claus beard was the most prominent. The jolly look was replaced with small, cold eyes that gave me a shiver when he looked at me. The second man was the Stan Laurel to the plump Hardy on the other side of the room. He didn't have the soft innocent countenance of the comedic figure of renown. He looked like a mortician suffering a migraine. His eyes and mouth were tight, as if in pain. He's the only one of the two that spoke.

He pointed to the chained man.

"Meet Konstantyn Zielinski. He gave us interesting information once the cocktail kicked in."

I looked at Diesel's guy, then at him.

"Cocktail?"

"Physical torture is passé," he said. "Today we rely on pharmacology. Mostly modern derivatives of the KGB's SP17 truth serum."

Antonio held up his hand and the skinny Stan Laurel shut up.

"Konstantyn is a double agent," Antonio said. "He's been working with Diesel for years, but also gets paid by the wholesaler to keep them informed of all the gang's plans."

'That won't be a healthy position once Diesel finds out,' I said.

"He already knows. He's out taking care of business.'

"So, who put the price on our heads?"

"The Texmex gang. A local wholesale drug distributor supplied from the Cartel Del Noreste. Diesel was honest with everyone. He told them he was adding a new supplier from the far east, but with the expansion he had planned, it would not impact what he was currently moving for them. With the information from Konstantyn, they decided to steal Diesel's expansion plan, eliminate the middleman, and distribute more of their drugs themselves."

I stepped closer to Antonio.

"What does that have to do with us?"

"They thought I was a rep for the new supplier, and you were a crooked cop on the payroll. They sent the three amateurs to get us out of the picture. Diesel's idea to let one of them go back with the message not to mess with us backfired. They panicked and put a price on us and on Diesel."

"They should have stuck to their wholesale business," I said. 'To quote Rumi, "Greed makes man blind and foolish, and makes him easy prey for death".'

"Well, Diesel's posse is working at that," Antonio said. "We picked this mutt up several hours ago. Diesel should call in soon. In the meantime, we stay off the streets."

We left Laurel and Hardy in the basement dungeon. They had instructions to deliver the traitor to Diesel after this was all over.

We went upstairs and feigned a serious workout. The gym's cameras would serve as a basis for our whereabouts while vengeance roamed the street.

Diesel called forty minutes later. Antonio put him on speaker.

"We cleaned up the five garbage bags from behind the restaurant. They're in a landfill. One bag we recycled. Everything is clean now."

Antonio gave me a thumb up sign.

"Wash up and head home," he said.

I headed to the showers, knowing that he had more to say to Diesel, but it was probably something that I shouldn't know about.

Before leaving, I warned Antonio.

'Pat knows I was in a shootout. She was surprisingly upset that I was flippant about it, to the point of tears. Since we've been living together, we've gotten closer. She doesn't know that there was a price on my head. Let's keep it like that.

Antonio nodded yes, then corrected me.

"Our heads."

FORTY- TWO

Pat gave me a summary of her meeting with the law firm that offered her the internship. We had a few bites and a glass of Bernard-Massard bubbly, but we were both too tired for more than that.

Next morning, I would have easily and happily accompanied Pat in some extra snooze time and wake up an hour later, but someone rudely reminded me of my cat servant duties. I fed Crackers, let him out and picked up the shreds of the two geometric printed paper napkins I had left on the kitchen counter from last night's midnight snack. I found the cork from the bubbly wine floating in my toilet bowl. How my feline managed that, I'll never know.

I made a stack of blueberry pancakes, gobbled a few and left a stack for Pat in the refrigerator with her 50% fewer calories of light maple syrup next to the note on how to reheat them so they remain soft and fluffy.

* * *

I got to the gym early. This was the last day of the week that I'd do my training. I normally took a break during the weekend.

Antonio trounced the speed bag at a rate that made his gloved fists a mere blur. He nodded hello and continued his routine.

I changed into my gym clothes, did my warm-up exercises, and an hour and a quarter of weights.

I met Antonio in his office after my shower.

"So I guess Diesel was not the villain after all," I said.

"Yea, but he ran a loose ship. This guy had been double-crossing him for years. One of my war buddies shadowed him for a day and found him meeting with the second in command of the wholesaler's gang. Didn't look right. We picked him up and questioned him. Problem solved."

"In Diesel's defense, he's part of a motorcycle gang. Your friends have been in the mercenary business longer than Diesel has been alive," I said.

'Not the point Robert, if you're in any operation, be a professional, don't do anything half-assed. It'll catch up with you. In my business, it was lethal.

"Have to agree with you on that. Every time I wasn't on my best game, I wound up in the hospital.'

I changed our discourse to a nicer subject.

"I haven't seen your girlfriend in a while. You guys still good?"

"Carol and I are real good. She's not at the restaurant very often. I put her in charge of the home. She works late and loves every minute. It seems to make amends for her not being able to help her abused twin sister," Antonio said.

"I'll carry the pain of that hostage situation to my grave," I said.

"You couldn't have saved her. Her boyfriend was a total nut case. You got two other women out before all hell broke loose. Let it go."

"I don't let it get to me. It just pops up when I get into a similar situation. If Nestruck hadn't obeyed my instructions when he was beating his wife. I would have pulled on him without remorse," I said.

"Want breakfast?" Antonio asked.

"Had a couple of pancakes early this morning. Those calories are long gone."

We ordered breakfast from a nearby restaurant. I gave the delivery boy a handsome tip.

We ate slowly and philosophized about the changes in today's society. Mostly the poor way they ran the country. Canada, such a beautiful country, with so much potential and so badly managed, was the consensus. I left with a full stomach, but none the wiser about the sad state of politics in Canada.

I called Dobson to give him the info I had from Lawyer Galkin. It went directly to voice mail. He's often called to testify in court on technical issues. I left the names that our mystery lady was using and asked him to do a search with both of them. He called me back an hour later. Told me he'd work on the mystery lady, and he signed off on the analysis report of the Nestruck crime scene. They had not found other fingerprints than those expected.

It was Friday afternoon. I declared the weekend officially started, and headed home.

* * *

I was flabbergasted to find Crackers waiting at the patio door with a less furry miniature copy of himself standing at his right.

"Somebody had an affair six or seven months ago. It's come back to haunt you, hasn't it?"

I slid open the door. Crackers sauntered in as if he was proud of himself. The kitten hesitated at crossing the doorsill. I picked it up, peeked under its tail, and placed it next to the food bowl. Crackers pulled back and let his daughter eat his favorite fishy mix. I added some soft meat from a new can and they both dived in.

I wasn't certain of what reaction I'd get from Pat about a fresh addition to the family. Personally, I mentally signed the kitten adoption papers when I saw Crackers lick the little fur ball clean after their meal.

An hour later, Pat came in, dropped her book-filled backpack to the floor, took one surprised look at her favorite sand colored living room chair and froze in place. The one that Crackers is not supposed to be on. He wasn't, but the mini cat was.

"Holy saints in heaven, what have we here?"

She picked up the kitten to eye level. It hugged her cheeks and licked the tip of her nose. Well, that was that. We had an addition to the household. She put the kitten in front of Crackers.

"I guess this is yours. I don't care how cute he is, not on this chair, NOT on this chair."

Crackers understood the tone of voice. He escaped down the hall toward the kitchen, the kitten following close behind. I corrected Pat's terminology.

"She," I said. "They were both sitting at attention on the balcony when I came home.

I think she's four or five months old. I let them in and fed them. There's a big family resemblance to our furry fiend."

"We're often out of the house. It's not good for a cat to be alone. I'd not be against keeping it—her. I'll do a net search to see if a neighbor lost a kitten before we claim it," Pat said.

"Spoken like a true lawyer," I said.

I prepared supper while Pat did her computer thing. She found a lady that was giving the litter of five away for adoption. She put them out in a big box on the balcony with the mom for some fresh air while she vacuumed the house. When she came back, the only black kitten in the bunch had disappeared. She was glad it was safe with us.

"Crackers is guilty of catnapping, but the lady is okay with us having the kitten," Pat declared as we sat down for supper.

We chatted about our day while watching the cats frolic at play, attacking each other from under the kitchen chairs.

"We can't sleep in tomorrow morning. I have instructions from your uncle to be at a gallery on Sherbrooke Street. A cousin of yours is having a showing. He expects us at the ten o'clock opening," I said.

"Francine. Her paintings are *feckin* brilliant."

I guessed I had something to look forward to.

FORTY- THREE

My morning started on the wrong foot. The one that stepped in cat poop at my side of the bed. I scooped it up with a tissue, picked up mini-Crackers by the scruff of the neck and deposited both packages into the big litter box in the corner of my bathroom. When Crackers came rushing in, I pointed to the bewildered kitten sniffing at her recent present. Maine Coons must have psychic talents. Crackers diligently demonstrated the proper bathroom etiquette to his offspring.

I prepared breakfast, showered, and dressed while being hampered by the always underfoot kitten who seemed mesmerized by my feet, the bath towel, my socks, or anything that moved in the slightest. I had inherited a fully grown Crackers on one of my cases. I had skipped the frolic kitten stage.

* * *

It disappointed Crackers that we didn't let him out on his regular morning critter hunt. We volunteered him for kitten sitting duties and left both of them indoors. I hoped we'd have a home to come back to.

We got to the gallery five minutes before the opening. There were already twenty plus people waiting in the venue's foyer. We met my boss Pat's uncle, wife Irene, artist Francine and her current boyfriend and agent Juan. Pat did the introductions on our side. The artistic cousin looked artsy with frizzed blue streaked hair and wore some type of light open weave serape over black leggings and a simple pale blue blouse. The long-haired five o'clock shadowed Juan was in a business suit and looked like a hungry real estate salesman, overly friendly, and out to make a sale.

We entered as a group. The place was packed twenty minutes later. Pat stuck with aunt Irene while I roamed the two rooms dedicated to Francine's oil paintings. I quickly understood Pat's 'feckin brilliant' comment.

The artist had captured sunlight in all of her works. Whether a still life or a person in a windowed room, using a play of light and shadow, objects and subjects appeared in three dimensions.

O'Neil sidled up to me as I was admiring a rendering of a ballet dancer at practice.

"Apart from a ream of paper work from on-the-scene officers at a street shoot out, I haven't had any recent reports on your cases," he said. "Am I to presume you're on a non-authorized vacation?"

"Not at all. Both the cold case Jane Doe murder and the biker found in the car trunk at the airport are related. I've got new clues and I expect to solve both shortly," I boasted.

"I'm pleased you have new clues. Where do I find that information in our records and files?"

I ignored the jibe, fished my phone out of my jacket pocket, and swiped to my picture file.

"I'm looking for this woman as a material witness. I found the name and alias she's using. Dobson is searching databases. I expect a break soon."

O'Neil unexpectedly grabbed the phone out of my hand and looked at Claudia's picture closely.

"I've seen this woman," he said loudly.

I turned head on to face him.

"You serious?"

"She was in the waiting area to see the same oncologist as Irene. She was two chairs away from me earlier this week."

"I'll have to give you credit for solving my cases," I said. "We'll have to collaborate on the report."

"The Cedar's oncology clinic begins treatment at eight thirty on Monday morning. Get your ass there when it opens. You're welcome," O'Neil said.

His mustache ends were slightly curled up. I also had a smile.

FORTY- FOUR

The weekend zipped by like they always do. The kitten had claimed her place in our house and Crackers was teaching her to push anything moveable from a bureau, desk, or shelf to the floor while maintaining a completely innocent look.

Monday asserted its reputation as the not-best day of the week with a morning shower. The weather guessers predicted a hot, overcast, humid day with intermittent showers until midnight when Tuesday would bring better prognostics.

I was up earlier than the cats. I fed them. I had showered, breakfast was done, jeans, jacket, and shoulder rig on. I was ready to find my mystery lady. I was sure she would provide me with the decisive clues to the murders.

* * *

I arrived at the McGill University Health Center at eight forty-two. A blue jacket volunteer lady at the entrance directed me to the second-floor wing of the Cedars Cancer Center.

Monitors on both sides of a waiting area posted the abridged names of patients and showed their required destination. The second name on the screen was Claudette Fe———Salle B4—Treatment room B4.

At my far left, a dark-haired woman her back to me, but much resembling my target entered the door to the treatment center. I rushed to catch up to her. I missed the closing door that locked behind her.

I returned to the reception area, flashed my badge, and told a nurse that I had to speak to the woman that just entered the treatment area.

"I don't care if you're the Pope. The patients are all immunocompromised. Go to the guard station and get a mask."

I rushed to the rent-a-guard desk.

"I need a mask to enter the treatment area. The nurse told me you'd give me one."

"Are you a patient?"

"No, I need to speak to a woman in treatment."

"Can't give you a mask if you're not a patient."

My lack of patience got the better of me. I did the badge flip move and took out my handcuffs from my back pocket.

"You have thirty seconds to give me a mask or I'll arrest you for interfering with a murder investigation."

I guess he'd suffered worse comments from patients frustrated with wait times and red tape.

His eyes laughed at me. The white appeared to sparkle in contrast to his dark complexion. He rose slowly from his seat, all six-foot-six of him.

"Take a deep breath and relax, buddy."

He pulled out a blue tinted paper mask from the box on his desk and handed it to me in slow motion.

"Have a good day," he said.

I mumbled, "Thanks, you too."

Wearing my mask, I went back to the reception desk. I answered no to a list of questions asking if I had traveled to a farm or if I had any symptoms of disease. Finally, approved for entry. Another nurse came to card the door open and let be in.

Along the left corridor, I followed the signs to room B4. It was one of many rooms that had the same layout. Raised lazy boy type recliners set in spaces along the walls. The far wall was large windows at ground level looking over the grass park at the rear of the hospital complex. It was still raining outside.

At the open entrance to the treatment room was a nurses' station against a waist-high wall. I skirted the desk and monitor station.

Installed in the first chair, my mystery lady wore a short-sleeved printed blouse with small light blue polka dots over an off-white base. She was plugged into an I.V. dripping a saline solution from a Y connection on the tube with something else from red labelled half-sized bag also on the pole. The clear plastic conduit fed through some machine next to her into her right arm. A printed sticker on the smaller bag showed a hospital code and her name as Claudette Fey.

I did my left-handed badge flip move and sat on the chair next to her. In light of the medical situation she appeared to be in, my intention was to question her gently.

"Good morning, Claudia. The blue on your blouse is the same shade as the outline on your butterfly tattoo. I have a fashionista friend that would compliment you."

Her reaction was not what I expected. She seemed to freeze for a few seconds, then tears ran down her cheeks.

"You must be a good detective. I expected more time." She spoke with a hint of a Spanish accent. She gave a little shudder and continued. "I don't want to die in prison."

I was confused and hesitated to answer. I picked up on her comment.

"I'm the best in the department. Why don't you tell me your story? We'll take it from there."

I pressed the record button on my phone's app.

FORTY- FIVE

Her sad story unfolded slowly. The flow of tears had subsided. I let her tell it at her own pace. She spoke softly, taking in a deep breath after each sentence. When a nurse came to see if Claudia was okay, she waved her away.

"I was visiting Montreal during Pride Week and met Roxanne in a downtown bar. *Fue amor a prima vista.*"

"I know the feeling. It was love at first sight with *my* redhead," I said.

She managed a little smile.

"Roxanne was a secretive person. I never knew much about her history or her family. I only found out her family was famous and wealthy when we went to her parents funeral. She was sad for weeks.

When we came back to Canada, we mostly stayed home. I understood. I'd been through something similar."

I nodded and gave her all my attention.

"With Monica?"

"You know everything?" She said.

I was still unsure where this interview was heading.

"Nearly, I need you to fill in the blanks," I lied.

She continued with her story with Roxanne.

"Roxy bought me a motorcycle on my birthday end of last April. I love the feeling of freedom and pushing fast through the wind. It feels like flying. I hadn't driven since the accident. I was following Monica when she hit a blown truck tire in a bend. She went over the railing. It took me a year to get over the event. I told Roxy I'd think about riding it when I felt better. She was not happy that I wasn't jumping for joy at her gift."

I couldn't let her ramble on. I wanted her to move ahead to the day Roxanne disappeared.

"Did Roxanne disappear shortly after the bike purchase?" I said.

Claudia hesitated a few seconds at my interruption.

"Maybe two weeks or so after, she told me about an afternoon meeting to settle something. I told her I'd have supper for her when she came back. She said great but seemed brusque and worried."

"What happened?"

"She never showed up. For the first hours, I thought she had met someone else and was punishing me for snubbing her present."

"Was that her style?"

"No, she was secretive, but very warm and tender," Claudia said. "You really must be a good detective. Even with all my precautions, it only took you a few weeks to find me. Me, I checked the hospitals for days, then spent months and months going to friends, to clubs, and the restaurants we used to hang out at, before I figured it had to do with the bike sale."

"You didn't report her as a missing person?" I said.

"My visa expired ages ago. I'm illegal."

I phrased my question carefully. I now knew where this conversation was going, and it saddened me.

"What was your final clue to what happened to Roxanne?"

"A total fluke. After weeks of hanging in biker bars. I met a guy high on coke and booze. When he tried to paw me, I told him I was gay. He said he knew a biker that bragged about choking a lesbian because she refused to sleep with him. He gave me the name. It was the same as the man that sold her my bike. Frank Diorio."

"In my business, I dig and dig and sometimes the clue finds me," I said. "What's the punch line, Claudia?"

"You know I left him at the airport. My father was the best butcher in the town of Salta. I learned to handle knives from a young age. It was quick. I wish I could have killed him more than once."

I didn't show any reaction to her admission.

"Speaking of unpleasant things, what's your diagnostic?" I said.

"Advanced fourth grade metastatic pancreatic cancer. The treatment is mostly for slowing down the progression and to reduce the pain. They gave me three to four months."

"I'm really sorry to hear this, Claudia. When did you find out?"

"Two weeks ago. I knew something was wrong months ago, but I was busy with my hunt."

The tears started again.

"I'm I under arrest? I can't die in prison."

I had done some bad things in my life. Sometimes I'd try to balance it out with a good deed. Her determined hunt for Roxanne's killer hit home painfully. I knew I would have done the same for anyone that would hurt Pat.

"You took care of dealing justice for Roxanne, and Karma has taken care of your punishment. I don't think that a trial will serve anything."

"You're not going to arrest me?"

"Don't tell anyone about this meeting. Officially, I haven't found you yet," I said. "I need to know where you're staying. I want your passport, your U.S. driver's license, a number where I can reach you, and the name and description of the man you met in the bar that gave you the information on Diorio. I'll see what I can do. I'll call you tomorrow."

"I'm traveling light. I have everything in my purse."

She gave me her documents, and I gave her my card.

I squeezed her hand and left her in peace.

FORTY- SIX

In the days following my visit to the oncology center, I got a sworn notarized statement from Claudia's contact, Carl 'Baby' Bergeron, relating to his conversation with Frank Diorio when he boasted of killing a gay woman. The lab had checked the samples taken from Diorio and Roxanne, proving they had intercourse. Although Frank would have deserved it, we couldn't charge him with the murder. A dead person cannot defend himself, ergo, no possibility of a fair trial. However, what I had was enough to complete my file and close that case.

For Diorio's murder, I had reciprocated our lunch meeting with my boss at the circular restaurant. I chanced telling O'Neil Claudia's story. He was receptive to my outside of normal procedures plan. Probably because of having lived through Irene's bout with the big C.

Claudia was currently under 'house arrest' as a material witness pending reams of paperwork slowly making their way between Canada immigration, the Argentine government, and our judicial system. We expected results in several months. I had installed her in the big room on the top floor of the home for abused women. We normally had a nurse on call. We added two full-time nurses to provide palliative care and assist Claudia with her treatments and medication.

It was the first week of May when I next visited the home. Carol buzzed me in and met me in the foyer.

"This is a surprise. You haven't been here in weeks," she said.

"Busy chasing bandits and fixing up the new house."

"How's Pat? I'm planning to have lunch with her next week. I haven't called her yet."

"She's very busy with her law courses. I'm sure she'd love a break."

"You here for Doctor Charlotte?" Carol said, "she brought us a support German Shepard from her clinic. It's helped the women when they take a walk. They now feel protected. Everybody loves Nosey. Charlotte's moving day is next Friday. She found a new apartment."

"Yes, I heard. She didn't want to stay in her old place with all the bad vibes attached to it. I'm here for Claudia," I said.

"Not bad news, I hope."

"Nope, good news."

* * *

Claudia's room door was open. I knocked on the frame. She put down her book and gave me a sideways nod.

"Not bad news, I hope."

"No. Everybody is asking the same question. Does my face indicate bad news?" I said.

"No, but you always look so serious." She pointed to the chair beside the bed. "Sit."

I read the title of the face up book at her side.

"Foley the Spy Who Saved ten thousand Jews. Interesting?"

"True story. I'm at the end of my life. The biggest regret I have is not helping more people during my stay on the planet."

"You may soon be able to. A lawyer will come tomorrow. You have papers to sign," I said.

"For my story that you recorded?"

"No, that's a deathbed confession that I'll date in due time. No, he's here with good news. Roxanne loved and appreciated you more than you knew. She changed her will after you married her. You inherit most of her estate. Eight million dollars, to be precise."

"*Mierda! Subirsele la mostaza.*"

"Although I don't know more than three words in Spanish, I can tell that you're not happy with the news," I said.

"A Spanish expression, I've got mustard tossed in my face. I'm pissed I won't have time to enjoy the windfall," Claudia said. "I've been very well treated here. Can I donate something?"

"You're free to do as you wish. I don't want to influence you. I inherited a fair sum from my ex-wife. I took it and opened this place. I had seen too many abused women when I was a cop on the beat."

"I thought it was Carol's dangerous-looking boyfriend that opened this home," Claudia said.

"He's a good friend. Antonio takes care of everything with Carol. He told me you're helping all the women here. Your tenacity going after your wife's killer, your brave attitude facing a terminal diagnostic, and your empathy to listen to the other women here, has made them put their own problems in perspective. Your stay here may give many the will and courage to face a new life, even if they are back to square one. You're a cathartic inspiration."

I brought tears to her eyes. I wasn't sure if they were happy or sad.

Claudia had found her peace. She was surrounded by women who cared for her and who spoke the secret language of inner feelings and of empathy that men will probably never comprehend or properly emulate.

On my way out, I met the wide furry black and tan support mascot. When she jammed her muzzle into my crotch, I figured out why they had named her Nosey.

EPILOGUE

Claudia beat the doctor's expectations. The thirtieth of October, she passed to another realm in her sleep. Carol called that morning to give me the sad news and told me Claudia had left me an important note.

I brushed an inch of snow off my Jeep. Winter had given us an early sample of what was to come. Across the street three kids were tossing snow at each other. Laughing, running, and jumping. That there was one less person on the planet bothered no one but me.

* * *

I had a lump in my throat when I read Claudia's handwritten note. She had fought the cancer till the end and had fulfilled her hope of helping people while she was among us. She had given Roxanne's trust lawyer's instructions to donate two million dollars to our home to expand the facilities. Another two million had gone to cancer research. She had provided a nice sum for Sondra and Helen, the two nurses that took care of her in the last months. Her note did not divulge what happened to the balance of the remaining four million.

I had orders to bury her ashes with Roxanne in the Saint John family plot in Bolton. She confirmed the only remaining family member, Roxanne's brother; had approved it.

During Pat's November school break, we took a flight to England to execute Claudia's wishes. At the cemetery, the director confirmed the arrangements. She took charge of the process. On the following chilly but sunny day, we were the only two at the simple ceremony.

Since we were in the United Kingdom, we took advantage of the trip to puddle jump to Ireland.

Pat reveled in showing me Dublin's charms. She planned a meeting so I could meet her older brothers. We had a man-to-man discussion in the hotel bar while Pat changed for supper. They both looked like younger and tougher copies of her uncle, my boss. Conor had the military short haircut and the same square jaw as the uncle, but without a mustache. He was the district superintendent of the Garda in the northwest district, stationed in Castlebar some three hours' drive northwest of Dublin. The elder, James, had a rounder, softer face but cold eyes the color of which reminded me of the clear blue of an iceberg. He was a warrant officer in the Royal Irish Regiment. I didn't get any other details from him.

After the first four minutes of chit-chat, I got the first serious question.

"I'm about asking you when you're going to make an honest woman of our sister."

"Conor, I mentioned marriage a year ago," I said. "Her reply was if it isn't broken, don't fix it."

"Maybe time to ask her again."

"That's a good suggestion. I'll wait till we're back home to ask her."

James peered at me from over the rim of his pint.

"Wasn't a suggestion."

"Ah, I'll best take it under serious advisement."

They both burst out laughing.

"We're just codding you. She seems perfectly happy," James said.

I had yet to get used to Irish humor.

The thought of marriage stayed with me. I was enjoying the trip but looked forward to home and a new adventure.

###

NOTE FROM THE AUTHOR

Word-of-mouth is critical for any author to succeed.

If you enjoyed the book, please leave a comment or review. Even if it's just a sentence or two. It would make all the difference and I would appreciate it very much.

kentnovelist@gmail.com

Thanks.

Michael Kent

Michael Kent is a retired international management and coaching consultant. Contrary to his technical writing, his fiction always has a tinge of humor and a special twist to the tale.

A native of Montreal, he is bilingual, often speaking French and English in the same sentence. Years as a private pilot, avid reading, and extensive traveling, have generated a storehouse of plots and stories to be shared with the world. A member of Canadian Crime Writers, and Sisters in Crime, he is also active with Writers on the net, Writers Village University, and The Next Big Writer.

http://www.kentwriter.com/

The Lieutenant Beaudry series:

Blood tail

Folded dreams

Twice dead

Tainted Evidence

Bank Shot

Dead Run

Deadly Storm

Dead End Ride

The Bereaved *

* Not yet in print

LINK TO THE BEAUDRY MYSTERY COLLECTION

Ottawa Review of Books – Jim Napier

The Lieutenant Beaudry novels will appeal to fans of the hard-boiled school: a stylistic amalgam of Mickey Spillane, Robert Crais, and Robert B. Parker. Colorful, fast-paced action novels set in multicultural Montreal. Author Kent's protagonist goes about his job without worrying about being politically correct or polishing the police department's public image. Beaudry is a straight shooter in the literal sense of the word. With help from friends on both sides of the badge, he has the best case closed record in the homicide department. He's a good cop who cherishes his Irish live-in girlfriend, puts up with his crazy Main Coon cat and lives life on his own terms. The series provides a cracking good read, one that does not disappoint.